# THE COWBOY AND THE CHAMPION

CHRISTIAN CONTEMPORARY WESTERN ROMANCE

BRUSH CREEK COWBOYS ROMANCE, BOOK 5
BOOK FIVE

LIZ ISAACSON

Copyright © 2020 by Elana Johnson, writing as Liz Isaacson

All rights reserved.

No part of this book may be reproduced in any form or by any electronic or mechanical means, including information storage and retrieval systems, without written permission from the author, except for the use of brief quotations in a book review.

ISBN-13: 978-1638760856

"And the Lord shall guide thee continually, and satisfy thy soul in drought, and make fat thy bones: and thou shalt be like a watered garden, and like a spring of water, whose waters fail not."

Isaiah 58:11

# Chapter 1

"Landon?" Emmett Graves entered the homestead at Brush Creek Horse Ranch just after five o'clock on a Friday afternoon. He'd been told by the foreman that the owner wanted to see him before the weekend. So here he was.

Landon, apparently, was not at the homestead, as Megan poked her head up from the kitchen cabinets where she crouched. "Hey, Emmett." She gave him a smile and disappeared again.

He moved through the living room, past a set of stairs that went down, and into the kitchen, where he found Megan organizing plastic storage containers and nesting them inside each other.

"Where's Landon?"

"He hasn't come in from the ranch yet." She glanced up at him. "What do you need?"

"He wanted me to stop by." A sense of urgency trickled through Emmett. He wanted to shower, grab something to eat, and get down to town. The country line dances had been going for a couple of weeks now, and he'd enjoyed himself at them.

"I'll text him." She stood and sent a message to her husband. "You goin' dancin' tonight?"

He laughed. "Don't talk like a cowboy," he said. "You can't even pull it off."

"Yes, I can." She slugged him in the shoulder. "So are you going?"

"Yep."

"You meet anyone down there?"

"Oh, don't start on me." Emmett groaned. "Between you and Tess it's a miracle I don't have a date every other night."

"Do you want a date every other night?" Megan's dark eyes glittered. "Because I know a lot of women that would be interested."

"*I'm* not interested," Emmett said. Megan tilted her head and looked at him with curiosity, but Landon entered the house through the French doors, saving Emmett from trying to explain.

*Trying* to explain was all he could do. No one really understood his aversion to women —not even Emmett himself. All he knew was that women couldn't be trusted. They didn't stick around when things got hard. His momma had left when he was twelve, and he hadn't heard from her since.

His father had been married and divorced three times, and both of Emmett's older brothers had endured divorces as well.

*No thank you*, Emmett thought as Landon washed his hands.

The fact that the owner hadn't said anything upon his arrival set Emmett's alert on high. "Ted said you wanted to see me before the weekend," he said.

"Right," Landon said, exchanging a glance with Megan. He sighed, further worrying Emmett.

"I've hired another trainer."

"That's great," Emmett said, trying to find the hidden meaning in the words. Or hear words Landon hadn't said at all.

"They'll be doing barrel racing as well. I need you to train them."

An icy wind swept through Emmett. "*They'll* be doing barrel racing? What will I be doing then?"

"Barrel racing."

Emmett's eyebrows pinched together. "So you'll have two barrel racing trainers?"

"For a while."

Emmett straightened his square shoulders. He wasn't as tall as Landon or some of the other cowboys on the ranch, but he could hold his own. "Am I being fired?"

"Of course not." Landon looked at Megan again, who came to stand at his side. A flash of resentment for their relationship stole through Emmett. At the same time, he envied them. "I'm just doin' a favor for a friend, and I need you to show them the ropes."

"When is this happening?"

"Monday." Landon held perfectly still, a tactic Emmett had seen him use before. It exuded confidence and the message that he wasn't going to budge on the topic at hand.

Emmett admitted defeat with an exaggerated sigh. "Fine. Is that all?"

"That's all. Just be here at the homestead at seven sharp on Monday morning."

Emmett saluted Landon, who rolled his eyes and said, "Get outta here."

———

WITH HIS TEETH brushed and his dark hair still a bit damp and curling on the ends, Emmett set his sights down the canyon. The temperature improved by a few degrees as he left the higher elevations behind. The dances were held at Oxbow Park, the largest outdoor venue Brush Creek had to offer.

The days were getting longer now that May was half over, and Emmett parked with several minutes of sunlight left. He made his way past the playground to a large pavilion which had been emptied of all the tables. Music pumped from the lit space, the kind of country twang that brought a quick smile to Emmett's face.

He didn't join the throng of people already on the cement dance floor right away. He stuck to the edges, checking out the dancers and finding his groove with the music. He chewed his arctic ice gum with vigor, his anticipation of expending some extra energy on the dance floor amping up.

"Hey, Emmett." A blonde-haired woman walked by, but Emmett barely glanced at her as he returned the greeting. He really wasn't interested in anything long-term with a female. But spending an evening dancing with one was perfectly fine.

He merged into the crowd during the song transition,

finding himself right next to a tall, curvy woman wearing jeans that went on forever. It was the jeans that should've tipped him off. Most of the other women there wore flirty little dresses, not jeans, black cowgirl boots, and a blouse the color of clouds.

He tapped the heel of his boot, then the toe, launching himself fully into the line dance. The redhead next to him had clearly missed the last several years of line dances, because she fumbled all over the place, even coming close to backing into him a time or two.

He chuckled and when the song ended, he said, "When's the last time you line danced?"

She trained her dazzling hazel eyes on him, and Emmett thought he might be really interested in dating her. "It's been a while," she admitted. Her gaze slid down his body and back to his cowboy hat, where her lip curled.

She had skin that had spent plenty of time in the sun. Freckles dotted her nose and cheeks, and her hair had to be naturally curly.

"I don't think we've met," he said. "I'm Emmett."

"We haven't." The woman turned and pushed her way through the crowd to a different section of the dance floor, leaving Emmett to stare after her.

He blinked and a laugh flew from his throat. Another song started, and Emmett kept his eye on the dancing disaster that was the redhead. Another man—sans cowboy hat—spoke to her, and she seemed perfectly warm with him.

Emmett's mood dampened, and he maneuvered toward the refreshment table. So what if that woman didn't like him? He wasn't looking for anyone either. He just thought if *he'd* nearly trampled someone, the least he could do was apologize. And if someone introduced themselves to him, his good Southern manners dictated that he introduce himself back.

The frustration over the nameless woman left him as he downed a cup of lemonade, the chill of it intensifying against the mint of his gum. He refilled his cup and faced the crowd again. There were lots of other women here to dance next to. He didn't need her.

He turned to put his nearly-full cup of lemonade in the trashcan but collided with another body. His grip on the plastic cup failed and the yellow liquid doused the woman he'd nearly knocked over.

Now her cloud-colored shirt looked like a dog had peed on it.

"I'm sorry," Emmett said as he picked up the empty cup and put it in his original target—the trashcan. He grabbed a fistful of napkins and started pawing at the woman's shirt.

She backed up and held up both of her hands. "Stop. Just...stop."

Emmett blinked, pure horror flowing through him at the distaste the woman wore on her face. Distaste for him. He wasn't sure what he'd done to make her dislike him so much—besides dumping ten ounces of ice cold lemonade down the front of her. But she'd seemed cold before then.

He forced a laugh and said, "So you can't dance, and I can't drink. Maybe we should both go home before we cause some real damage." He kept his genuine smile on his face. The smile he wore when he was trying to get something he wanted. The smile that always worked.

Almost always worked.

Because the redhead scoffed, spun away from him, and stomped out of the pavilion. Emmett followed her, pausing where the cement met the grass. "Wait!" he called. "I didn't get your number!"

She didn't even turn around, and Emmett faced the dance floor with a chuckle. That woman needed a chill pill, because it was only lemonade. It would come out in the wash, for crying out loud.

"You wanna dance?" The blonde parked herself in front of him, and Emmett figured *why not?*

"Sure." He gave that grin again, satisfied that it worked on some women. Human women, he thought as he scanned the darkness beyond the pavilion for the redhead. She was nowhere to be found, so he spun the blonde, and drank too much lemonade, and laughed good-naturedly until the dance ended near midnight.

# Chapter 2

Molly Brady scrubbed at her new silk shirt. The stubborn yellow stain didn't so much as turn a shade lighter. Oh, she could just kill that cowboy. First saying she couldn't dance and then dousing her in cold liquid the color of urine.

She finally gave up and lifted the shirt over her head. Molly had driven back to Beaverton in the wet shirt, and she had nothing to launder it with as she was staying in a hotel until she moved into her more permanent place tomorrow.

Running hot water in the bathroom sink, Molly submerged the shirt and cried out. Her hand turned an angry shade of red and she spun to the tub where she fumbled with the faucet, finally getting it on and turned to cold. She sighed as the water took out the heated sting from the sink.

Another issue caused by that cowboy. Molly was no stranger to cowboys, having spent the last eight years of her life surrounded by them. Traveling with them. Enduring their catcalls. Though the one at the dance had been cute—handsome even—the arrogant way he wore his dark brown cowboy hat and that crooked grin had gotten under her skin.

She knew men like him. Knew they only wanted one thing from her and it didn't end with an evening of dancing.

After a stalking altercation that had lasted almost a year, Molly had decided to leave the rodeo. Find somewhere she could go that no one knew her, and where she didn't have to worry about checking over her shoulder to make sure Clay Corwin wasn't there.

She changed into her pajamas, furious at herself for even going to the dance. She'd driven all the way from Nebraska today, and she was dead-dog tired. But she'd overheard some women talking about the dance while she picked up her calzone that night, and she'd thought *what the heck?*

Molly wasn't sure how often she'd get to the town of Brush Creek, and she thought she'd scope it out before she missed her chance. She didn't need long in a town to figure out its personality, as she'd traveled all over the country as she racked up wins in women's barrel racing.

She sighed, her mind far from her old life as she remembered the small-town charm of Brush Creek. She'd been having a great time until that light-eyed, dark-haired cowboy had ruined it.

With those negative memories driving away the anxious thoughts of the new life she was starting tomorrow, she fell asleep.

THE NEXT MORNING, Molly didn't get out of bed before dialing Brynn Bowman, the last woman who'd dominated the rodeo circuit. Molly had come on the scene in the last couple of years of Brynn's fame, and though she liked the other woman, Molly hadn't been sorry to see her go, because Molly could finally win without Brynn on the circuit.

She hadn't dreamed that her friendship with Brynn would be needed all these years later.

"Hey, Mols, what's up?" Brynn sounded chipper for so early in the morning, and Molly yawned.

"Just letting you know I'm in Utah."

"Going to meet Landon today?"

"Yeah." Molly chewed on her thumbnail. "Tell me again this is the right place for me."

Brynn sighed, and Molly imagined her tossing her dark braid over her shoulder and staring her down with her intense eyes. So much of Brynn reminded Molly of herself. "I wish I had a place for you here at Three Rivers. But I don't. I'm overbooked for horses, and I've been sending my leads to Landon for a few months now as it is."

"So he'll have work for me to do."

"He does, yes. Lots of it. And he's an honest guy. Hard worker. You'll be happy at Brush Creek."

Reassured, Molly sat up. "Thanks, Brynn." She didn't necessarily need the money, but she needed something to do. She'd briefly contemplated going home to Nebraska and staying, but once she'd gotten there, she knew she couldn't stay.

She hung up with Brynn and ran her fingers through her curls, glad she'd chosen to chop them after her retirement. There was only so much she could do with the naturally curly mass on her head, and sticking a bow in it and letting it flow over her shoulders had gained her a lot of admirers in the rodeo circuit.

They didn't know it took her a full forty minutes to comb out all the tangles and knots after a competition. They didn't know how frustrating and infuriating having all that hair was. And now she didn't have to worry about what her fans thought.

She seated her cowgirl hat on her head and carried her bag out to her truck. A short half-hour drive later, and she crested the hill that led to the horse ranch. Brilliant, blue sky filled the horizon before her, with lush green grass on both sides of the gravel road. A row of six cabins lined the lane to her right, with the homestead and all the other ranch buildings on the left.

Molly parked in front of the sidewalk that led to the front door. Drawing a deep breath, she closed the distance to the door and lifted her hand to ring the doorbell. The homestead at Brush Creek Horse Farm was exactly as Brynn had described. Upscale and quaint at the same time. Beautiful but functional too.

A dark-haired woman answered the door, and Molly felt an immediate kinship to her because of her naturally curly hair. "You must be Megan." Molly put on her best showmanship smile and shook the woman's hand. "I don't know how you keep your hair so long." She swiped off her hat. "I finally cut mine the day after I retired from the rodeo."

Megan laughed with her and asked her if she wanted coffee. Molly was already so jittery, so she passed.

"My husband is out back with our daughters. Let me grab him."

"Of course." Molly watched the other woman glide gracefully through the house to the French doors in the back. Once, Molly thought she'd be able to live in a homestead like this, raise children with a man she loved, be free from the worries and cares of life.

But now, she didn't want to be married, didn't want children, and didn't want anyone to know about the first two. She just needed to live her life in obscurity, the one behind the scenes instead of on the championship horse.

"Molly," Landon said, entering the house. "You made it."

"I did, sir."

He scoffed and waved away her formality. "No 'sir' here."

"He really does hate it," Megan added as she stroked the hair of a little girl who was probably five or six years old.

Molly's smile hitched into place. "Very well, Landon. I understand you have a place for me to live on the ranch?"

Landon's feet shifted. "Well, sort of. It's a temporary arrangement, but the only place I have for you right now is in the basement."

Molly blinked. Blinked again. "I'm sorry? The basement here at the homestead?"

"That's right." He flashed her a quick smile. "I have plans to add to Cabin Row, but the first one won't be finished until the end of the summer, at which time, you'll move in there." He gestured toward a set of steps off the living room that led down. "Do you want to check it out?"

"Sure." Molly made her voice bright and tried to force a measure of optimism into her step. The basement was spacious, with a living area at the bottom of the steps that held two couches, a television, and an exercise bike.

"Two bedrooms down here," Landon said. "Bathroom between them. There's a small kitchen here too, so you'll have everything you need."

Molly poked her head in one of the bedrooms, but it was unremarkable. The bathroom was standard. The kitchen was more like a kitchenette, but with her limited cooking abilities, it would do just fine. After all, a freezer was a freezer was a freezer, and the tiny one in this basement would hold her microwavable meals as well as any other she'd had in the past.

"It's great," she said, though she wished she had her own structure, with privacy and maybe a tall fence. "Is there a separate entrance?"

"No, unfortunately," Landon said. "But we won't be in your way."

"That's not what I'm worried about." She glanced at Megan, who'd come downstairs with them. "Don't y'all have three children?"

"They're used to people coming in and out," Megan said. "Honestly, you're not going to bother us at all."

Molly wasn't so sure of that, but she smiled and nodded, wondering if that would be all she did out here at Brush Creek.

"See you Monday morning," Landon said, guiding his wife back to the stairs and out of sight.

Monday came, and Molly had barely left her basement bachelorette pad. She'd gone to the grocery store in the evening on Saturday and for a walk on Sunday once she'd heard Landon and Megan leave the house.

But she couldn't hide away in the basement forever, so she ascended the steps a few minutes before seven. Two distinct male voices tickled her eardrums as she neared the top, and she stepped into the living area to find Landon talking to another man. He shifted, and Molly's world turned white around the edges.

Not just any other man. Oh, no. The very cowboy who'd ruined her shirt.

"You," she said, a healthy dose of venom in only three letters.

The dark-haired man switched his gaze to Molly and his mouth dropped open. He recovered quickly, and asked, "What are you doin' here?"

"What am *I* doin' here? I work here."

"You've met?" Landon asked, volleying his gaze between the two of them.

"Not really," the cowboy said, glaring. Molly had no idea what he had to be upset about. *She* was the one with a shirt the color of banana popsicles.

"Well, Emmett, this is Molly Brady. Molly, this is Emmett Graves. He's gonna be your trainer."

Molly closed her eyes and ground her teeth together, silently begging God to open a hole in the earth wide enough to swallow her whole. When she opened her eyes, arrogant, handsome Emmett Graves still stood there, grinning at her for all he was worth.

## Chapter 3

Emmett could mask a lot of emotions behind his smile, a weapon he used when he really wanted to stalk from the room and slam the door behind him. He should've known the leggy redhead was a cowgirl —he'd *known* there was something off about the clothes she wore to a country line dance.

"So she'll be shadowing you for a few weeks, and then I expect you to put her to work." Landon clapped Emmett on the shoulder, bringing him out of the staring contest with Molly. She finally looked away too, cocking one hip and folding her arms.

Landon left, probably because the tension in the homestead was explosive and he didn't want to get hit with any of the shrapnel. Megan hummed as she entered the kitchen with her two-year-old in her arms.

"Oh, good morning, you two. You've met?" She didn't seem to notice the thickness of the air or the fact that Emmett and Molly were still facing off. He didn't want to be the first to speak or move—or maybe he did. Take control of the situation.

Whatever. He sighed and turned toward Megan. "We've met." He went into the kitchen, fully expecting Molly to simply follow him. "Lunch today?"

"Pasta salad and grilled chicken."

"Gotta use up all those noodles you bought last fall, is that it?"

"Hey." She laughed when she met Emmett's eyes. "You never know what winter is going to be like here. If we'd been snowed in, you'd have been happy for all those noodles."

Emmett danced away from her as she waved a wooden spoon around. "I still am, Megs. Put the spoon down." He chuckled as he exited through the French doors, his mood buoyed up by the sunshine and crisp blue sky. He took in a deep breath—and got a noseful of fruity-floral perfume.

Molly. He glanced behind him to find her only half a step back. He groaned. "Come on then." He purposely walked at a swifter clip than he normally did, but Molly kept up with him just fine.

"Have you had a tour of the ranch?" he asked.

"No."

"Where are you livin'?" he asked as he paused next to the machinery shed.

"The basement."

Emmett openly stared at her. "Permanently?"

"Landon said he was going to expand Cabin Row. Said he commissioned someone named Blake to build a few more cabins."

This was the first Emmett had heard of an expansion project, but he didn't really need to know, though if Blake was going to be spending his work hours on construction, surely someone would have to pick up the slack on the farming side of the ranch's operation.

"Well, this here's the machinery shed. Has three bays. Landon's fairly handy with cars and trucks. So am I, for that matter." He pointed to the building behind it. "Big shed there holds most of our smaller farming supplies." He started walking again. "Bigger machines here." He pointed to the swathers, balers, tractors, mowers, and trailers.

"We don't do much with farming, do we?"

"During planting and harvesting, yes. The Horse Ranch relies on what we can grow ourselves, or things get a little pricey. Blake—who's going to build your cabin—manages and oversees all the farming operations, but everyone helps for a few days during peak times."

She swallowed and nodded, her eyes never leaving the giant machines parked next to the bays. Emmett suppressed his smile, instead giving her a judgmental look that she ignored.

"Anyway," Emmett said. "The horse barn is over here. We have about twenty horses at any given time, and Landon schedules us in the pastures, the outdoor arena, or the indoor training facility. Our barn holds twenty-five horses, and I've heard Landon talking about expanding it."

"The ranch must be doing well," Molly said, and Emmett was a touch surprised at the awe and kindness in her voice.

"Must be," Emmett said. "He's never hired a new

trainer before. There's always been him, five of us, and our farming manager."

"Six cabins across the street."

"All single occupied," Emmett said. "Well, except for the cowboys who've got families." He glanced through the budding trees at the row of cabins. One had bicycles leaning against the tree out front, and another had a stroller parked on the front porch.

"How many of them have families?" she asked.

Emmett's stomach twisted, though he couldn't identify why. "The foreman is married. Has two boys. His wife cuts hair. Our team roping trainer got married a couple of years ago, and they just had a baby last fall. Let's see...." Emmett entered the barn as he pretended to think. "Our bronc trainer is married, with a baby who's almost two now. And Blake, the farmer, is getting married in a month or so. His fiancé has three kids already."

"So there are other women here. Children."

"Yeah." Emmett smiled, though as he'd given his little speech on those who lived at the ranch, he'd realized that only he and Grant Ford, another cowboy who worked with cattle, were single. He'd once been in the majority, and now he wasn't.

It was his turn to swallow uncomfortably as he led Molly down the aisle toward the horses he was currently training. He stopped outside the stall, the brown horse with a strip of white down her nose, coming forward to greet him.

"Hey, Little Hurricane." He stroked the horse's nose. "She's got quite a personality, but she's coming along." He grinned at the horse and then turned around to the black horse who'd also come over. "That there's Brush Creek Beauty." He loved Beauty, and he tapped his forehead to hers.

Molly seemed comfortable around horses, at least. She stroked Hurricane's nose too and let the horse sniff her palm. She wore a smile—at least until she faced Emmett. Then the smile faded and her surly attitude returned.

"What brings you to Brush Creek?" Emmett asked. "Saddles and reins are down in the tack room." He nodded further down the aisle and led the way.

"I just retired from the rodeo circuit."

Emmett's step stuttered. "Oh yeah? Let me guess. You were a barrel racer." He managed to mostly keep the disgust from infusing his voice.

"You don't like barrel racers," she stated.

"I like 'em fine when they're here buying my horses. Otherwise...." He scanned her from her strawberry blonde cowgirl hat to her black boottips. "I could do without them."

"Now let me guess," she said, jumping in front of him and almost coming chest to chest with him. "You rode bulls."

He smirked at her, one half of his mouth quirking up. He smacked his arctic gum, glad she'd get a whiff of mint if she was going to be standing so close. His body hummed, but he couldn't tell if it was a good thing or not. "Wrong. Guess again."

"Hmm." She narrowed her eyes. "Only cowboys as arrogant as you ride bulls."

"Well, I didn't."

"You weren't even in the rodeo, then."

"Sure was, sweetheart."

"We must've been on the circuit at the same time then."

"Why's that?"

"You can't be that old."

"I retired seven years ago." Emmett stared her down, wishing she'd back up a step. The hum definitely wasn't a good one, and his fingers clenched.

"And I started eight years ago. So there was some definite overlap."

"A year," he said. "An old pro like me probably didn't pay attention to a rookie." *Especially a barrel racing rookie*, he added in his mind.

Her freckles stood out against her blush. "I'll find out what you competed in on the circuit."

"That's fine. I don't mind female fans." He stepped around her, his hip brushing into the stall to give her a wide enough berth, and entered the tack room. "Since you know how to ride, I'll let you go through the equipment here and get a saddle you think will work for Hurricane."

"Which horse is more practiced?" she asked, cramming herself into the small room with him.

Annoyance soared through him, almost clouding his judgment. "No one works with Beauty but me."

"Oh, you've got a crush on your pretty little horse, is that it?"

Emmett turned and faced her, even took a step closer to her. Satisfied when she shrunk back a step, he said, "That's right. And the other half of my heart belongs to my cat."

Her shoulders straightened and she lifted her chin,

completely unafraid of him. She really had survived well in the rodeo circuit. "Get your gear and meet me in the outdoor arena. We'll be there all week." Emmett grabbed his stuff and high-tailed it out of there before he could say or do something he'd regret later.

---

"All right, Beauty," Emmett said once he had his horse saddled and warmed up. He liked just riding around the outdoor arena, the gentle clopping of hooves therapeutic and the fresh breeze comforting.

When Molly entered the arena on Hurricane, Emmett's heart catapulted to the back of his throat. She was magnificent on a horse, her hands soft on the reins, her back straight and tall, her confidence oozing from her.

She smiled at him, and Emmett thought maybe he could tolerate her following him around for a few weeks. Then she could go off on her own. After all, if Landon really had more barrel racing business, he wouldn't allow two of them to train a horse at the same time.

She trotted Hurricane four feet from the fence line, around and around, just the way she'd surely warmed up her horse before a run. Emmett appreciated that she kept distance between them and that she knew what to do.

He pulled Beauty into the center of the arena and gestured for Molly to do the same with her horse. "So Hurricane is coming out wide on her turns. Sometimes she blows off that third barrel completely. I want you to get the barrels set up and walk 'er through the route. Keep her face loose; don't let her head come up on the second turn.

Make sure she's exactly four feet from that last barrel, and really set your weight on the outside so she'll come back in."

Molly nodded and loped her horse around the arena another time before dismounting and beginning to drag the barrels out to their positions.

He watched her for several seconds past appropriate. She had muscles in her arms and legs that he appreciated, along with those curvy hips that could steer a horse without much effort. He cleared his throat and looked away.

He wasn't happy about Molly's intrusion into his life. And the way she wore ice in every line of her face didn't help either. So she was strong, and capable, and beautiful. Didn't mean Emmett was getting warm fuzzies about her.

Leading Beauty out of the arena to the alley he'd constructed, he said, "We're gonna conquer this alley today." He led the horse to the entrance of the alley, and Beauty stopped. He jumped down and peered at her. "What's with this?"

Her refusal to run the alley was a new development that Emmett needed to sort out before he could advance her to the next part of her training. After all, if he couldn't even get the horse into the arena, there was no sense in making sure she could run the barrels.

He walked down the alley, leaving Beauty where she stood. He hummed to himself, hoping the horse had developed some anxiety that he could cure. He'd already had the vet and animal chiropractor out to the ranch, and Beauty wasn't showing any signs of soreness.

At the end of the alley, he unlatched the gate that led into the arena. Molly watched him, but he ignored her. He hummed as he went back, letting his fingers catch on every post until he returned to Beauty.

She'd never had a problem with noise—in fact he trained his hyper horses to deal with the distraction of crowd noise and focus on their runs. Some horses required a more gentle hand, and some needed to know their rider was there, solid in the saddle.

Emmett had tried different tactics last week to test Beauty's hypertension issues, and he'd found none. He gathered her reins and walked her down the alley. She plodded along behind him, but a snuffle and a head toss came about halfway down.

"Easy," he said, breaking his humming to soothe the horse.

"What's wrong with her?" Molly asked when Emmett made it into the arena.

"Nothing's wrong with her," Emmett said, instantly annoyed by the woman's quick judgment and slightly acidic tone. "She's just developed some anxiety about the alley." He reached up and stroked his fingers down her neck. "She'll be ready in no time. Come on, Beauty. Don't listen to the nasty barrel racer."

He shot a daggered look at Molly, who frowned and folded her arms, that hip jutting out. Emmett wondered how much she practiced that displeasured look, because she had it down.

"A *nasty barrel racer* is gonna have to ride her," Molly called as Emmett took Beauty through the alley in the opposite direction.

"But she won't have to deal with her anxiety," Emmett called back. "Because I'm going to train her up right," he added under his breath so Molly couldn't hear. He took the horse way out past the alley and turned her around.

"Slow and steady," he said, leading her back in. He kept a decent grip on the reins in both directions, glad when Molly had gotten on with training her own horse. He watched her lift her inside hand and put her weight on the outside, patting the horse's neck when it came all the way around the barrel and completed the turn.

He had to admit she knew what she was doing. Maybe she didn't know all the steps of taking a wild horse and training it into a champion, but she definitely had the skills to do it. If *she* was trained up right, she'd be churning out barrel racing horses by the end of the year.

For some reason that didn't sit well in Emmett's gut. He needed to release his own anxiety if he wanted to make any progress with Beauty today, so he lashed her to the post at the end of the alley and went back in the barn.

He stuffed one chocolate chip cookie in his mouth—his reward for dealing with Molly—and put three in his pocket. When he returned to Beauty, she nosed his jacket as if she could see through leather.

"Yep," he said. "You have to go down the alley—no snuffling, keep that head low—to get it." He undid her reins and dropped them, stepping into the alley and expecting the horse to follow.

She did, all the way to the end. Emmett smiled at her, praised her, and gave her a cookie. He repeated the process, this time with him on the outside of the alley. Beauty performed her job well, kept her head low, and went all the way into the arena. She even trotted over to the first barrel, as Emmett had already started teaching her the patterns and strides she needed to master.

He whistled through his teeth without thinking, and he got the desired result with Beauty. She turned and came back to him. Unfortunately, so did Hurricane, who Molly had been coaching through the patterns.

He gave Beauty a cookie and chuckled as Molly struggled to get Hurricane to return to the barrel patterns. The horse wouldn't though, as Emmett had trained it come to him on command.

He chuckled as Hurricane arrived and lifted his head over the fence, ready for his treat too. Emmett gave it to him along with an affectionate pat or two. Or ten. He wasn't counting.

Molly sighed in this hugely exaggerated way, and Emmett glanced at her sitting atop his horse like a queen.

"Sorry," he said, deciding to go for nice on this one. "I forgot about the effect my whistle has on him."

"It's fine." But her tone didn't suggest fine. It suggested absolutely, one-hundred percent not fine. Emmett watched her go and shook his head. She'd probably won a lot of championships. A rider as focused as she was had the discipline to train for hours a day for the fifteen-second run.

"C'mon Beauty," he said, moving back toward the beginning of the alley. "Try it with me on your back."

Again, he let the horse take the lead; he didn't guide her with the reins or his legs and feet. She made it to the end of the alley successfully, where Emmett found Molly on her phone. Familiar irritation rose within him. He'd always considered himself pretty easygoing; he liked to laugh; he enjoyed life. But something about this Molly woman had him all rankled.

"We don't bring our phones to work," he called, but she just maneuvered the horse so her back was fully toward him, her head still bent down at an angle that suggested she was still texting.

Emmett's blood ignited, and he set Beauty on a course to intercept Molly, the choice words he'd use to rebuke her piling up in his mind.

# Chapter 4

Molly's insides had gone cold at the text from her mother. She wasn't sure how her blood had continued to run for the past five minutes, frozen in her veins as it was.

*Daddy's in the hospital. The doctors are trying to stabilize him. I'll let you know what's going on when I know more.*

*Hospital* echoed in her mind. *Stabilize him.*

*What happened?* she'd texted. No answer.

*Are you with him?*

*What can I do?*

*Mom, call me when you can.*

She stared at her unanswered texts, her heart romping through her chest, taking prisoners. A sob built in her stomach and roared upward. All she could think to do from this far away was pray.

She closed her eyes, somewhat surprised at the slip of moisture that leaked from her left one, and sent a plea toward heaven. *Please save my father. Help calm my mother. Send comfort to me.*

Her first inclination when she'd received the news of her father's pancreatic cancer was to quit the rodeo circuit and return to Nebraska to be with him. He'd hear nothing of it, and he'd demanded she get back out there and finish the year a winner. She had, but she hadn't gone back. Not only because of Clay—though he was a huge factor—but because she wanted to be able to jet home at any time if her parents needed her.

But she didn't see how she could leave now. Not right when she'd just started at—

"No phones while training," Emmett barked as he appeared at her side. "The horses—" He brought his horse around as Molly blinked into the bright sunlight. "What's wrong?"

She didn't know the brute of a man could sound so tender. She met his eyes and found compassion there too. She didn't know how to make this version of Emmett line up with the one she'd formed in her mind.

"Are you okay?" he asked, only igniting the emotion in her chest and making the sob spurt from her mouth.

"Okay, not okay," he said. He dismounted, whipped his horse's reins around the top rung of the fence, and came to her side. "Get down, Molly."

She complied, only because her own brain didn't seem to be functioning. He eased the phone from her fingers and looked at it, but it had gone black.

Her legs trembled, and she hated this weakness in her. Hated feeling so helpless. She'd felt like this for a solid year as Clay stalked her, and she'd determined never to let anything affect her so negatively again.

"It's my dad," she said, gaining some measure of

control. A deep, deep breath, and she felt even calmer. "He's been taken to the hospital."

Emmett put one arm around her waist and pulled her into his chest. "I'm so sorry. An accident?"

She shook her head, trying to tame the tears and failing. "He has cancer." Her hands went around his broad back and she leaned into him. "He's been sick for a while." The words ghosted from her mouth, and she let Emmett hold her because it felt nice. Because she didn't want to be alone at this moment when her father might be dying. Because she was so, so tired of being so, so strong all the time.

Emmett hummed, the same way he had been when leading his horse down the alley, and the vibrations reverberated through his chest and into hers. She found comfort in them, oddly enough, and she finally found the well of strength she needed to stop the tears.

Now she had liquid pouring from every hole in her face though, and she didn't quite want to leave the warmth, safety, and security of Emmett's arms. From the bulk of his muscles, the man obviously worked out with more than just horses, and she enjoyed the musky, minty, mountainy scent of his shirt and neck and the way he held her tight without making it feel possessive.

Startled by her softening feelings toward him, she straightened and stepped back. "I'm sorry," she said, trying to wipe everything at once.

"Nothin' to be sorry about." He collected the reins of both horses and handed her phone back to her. "I'll be back in a few minutes. You wanna just wait here?"

She nodded and turned away from him as he took the horses back into the barn. She checked her phone, but her mother hadn't texted. Molly dialed her, the buzzing in her stomach so uncomfortable she leaned against the fence and doubled over.

No answer.

Molly reasoned that her mother was probably busy, filling out forms or talking to doctors. Or perhaps she didn't have great service in the waiting room where she was. Hospitals weren't great with that kind of thing, Molly knew.

She inhaled again, taking in more breath than she knew possible, stretching her chest until she thought she'd pop. She exhaled, willing her anxiety to leave with her breath. She did feel better afterward. Her mom would call when she could. That had to be enough for now.

Emmett returned, his light gray eyes still kind, still probing, and if Molly didn't know better, affectionate. She smiled at him. "Thank you."

"Did you hear back?" His gaze flickered to her phone and back to her face.

"Not yet."

"Let's go get some coffee," he said. "Megan always has some on."

Molly went with him, glad for a reason to keep both feet on the ground for a few minutes. "Does Megan regularly feed everyone?" Maybe she'd eat better than ever here at Brush Creek.

"Regularly?" Emmett considered the clear blue sky as if it held the answer to her question. "Yeah, I suppose she does. There's almost always lunch, but it's not always hot, especially in the summer. Do you like sandwiches?"

"Yeah, I like sandwiches," she said as she followed him

through the gate in the bricked wall surrounding the homestead.

"She does that a lot in the summer. If there isn't lunch at the homestead, we usually get a text." He paused next to the fire pit in the backyard. "You allergic to anything?"

"Cats," she said.

He blinked at her before tipping his head back and sending a booming laugh into the sky. Molly couldn't help the insta-smile that sprang to her lips. With so much happiness in the sound around her, she wanted to join in. "What's so funny?" she asked when he'd taken his laugh down to a chuckle.

"Wouldn't you know it? I own a cat."

"So?"

"So, just when I was startin' to think we could get along." He gazed at her for a moment past comfortable, a glint in his eyes she'd seen plenty of times. Desire. Heat. Interest.

He turned away from her before she could tell him she wasn't interested in dating. Not just him either. In general. Marriage held no allure for her, and she didn't want children.

She'd realized over the years that this opinion was semi-unpopular among women. The other barrel racers had cooed over the flowers Clay sent, while Molly had wanted to throw them away the moment they arrived.

One of her best friends in the circuit had confessed her jealousy over Brynn's marriage and subsequent family. Molly had pretended she wanted those things too. But she didn't. She'd wondered if it was because she was an only child and had always been fiercely independent, headstrong, and capable. She hadn't been able to reach a conclusion on that one. She had a close relationship with her parents, despite her travel schedule.

Other women lamented that there were no good cowboys to date. Molly didn't understand the desire for a cowboy at all. In her eyes, they were all manipulative, sneaky, jealous men. Of course, intellectually she knew this wasn't true. But the only one she'd ever allowed into her life had been like that, and she wasn't interested in a repeat of that heinous relationship. Therefore, all men who wore jeans or cowboy hats were out. At this point, she'd probably have to be seduced by a Scot wearing a kilt to even accept a date.

"You comin'?" Emmett called from inside the house. Molly tucked her past where it belonged—in the back of her mind—and hurried toward him.

---

A WALL of noise hit Molly when she stepped inside, and she blinked at all the babies. Fine, there were only 3 babies, and then two of the older girls she'd seen on Saturday. Seemed like a lot of women and children for ten o'clock in the morning, and Molly edged toward the much safer zone —the kitchen, where Emmett stood pouring black coffee into a double-sized mug. It read "We do things bigger in Texas," and a slip of a smile stole across her lips.

"What's goin' on here?" she asked as he pushed the mug toward her.

"Play group."

She blinked at him. How did someone like Emmett

know what a play group was? She squinted at him, but all these different pieces of him floated around him, unwilling or unable to make a cohesive picture.

He leaned forward and whispered, "You know, when all the ranch wives get together and let their kids play? Megan had Landon get the pool set up over the weekend. They're just waiting for it to get a bit warmer." He pointed to several bottles on the counter next to the stove. "Cream and sugar right there." He lifted his mug, drinking his coffee hot and black.

"Ranch wives?"

Emmett gestured toward the four women camped out in the living room, chattering like they hadn't seen another adult in weeks. "April, Megan, Tess, and Renee. I suppose Erin will join them once she and Blake are married." He peered at her like she'd lost her marbles. "Remember I said a bunch of the boys were married?" He nodded toward the women again. "Ranch wives."

"Like Real Housewives of Brush Creek Horse Ranch?"

A blonde with shorter hair than Molly entered the kitchen. "Oh, there's no drama," she said. "What a boring show that would be!" She laughed, sobering as she reached for Emmett's hat. "Emmett." She frowned at him. "Have you seen your hair?" She brushed at the curled ends of it, and a fierce rush of...jealousy roared through Molly.

She took a big gulp of her coffee and immediately choked. "Hot," she gasped, some of the liquid dribbling out of her mouth.

Emmett didn't seem to notice as he was swatting the blonde woman's hand away. "Leave me be, Tess. My hair's fine." He cast a sideways glance at Molly, who thankfully, had wiped away any evidence of coffee from the corners of her mouth. She gave him a closed-mouth smile because her tongue felt like she'd dipped it in hot wax.

She turned and poured a healthy dose of whatever creamer sat the closest. When she turned around, all the women had advanced into the kitchen. She felt very out of place among all the brunettes, but she shared her curly hair with Megan, and there was Tess, the blonde.

"You'd be so much more distinguished with a nice military cut," Tess persisted. She wouldn't give Emmett his hat back, and he wore a disgruntled look on his handsome face. He did possess a wealth of hair, and Molly quite liked how it curled along his neck.

"I'm not military," Emmett said.

"Too rebellious," one of the brunettes said.

"That's right," Emmett said. "And don't you forget it."

The women laughed, leaving Molly to think that Emmett wasn't rebellious at all. The conversation turned to the strawberry planting taking place that weekend, and since Molly knew even less about strawberry plants than she did about ranch wives, she remained silent.

"Are you going to go, Molly?" Tess asked. How the woman knew her name was a mystery to Molly. Of course, up here in this tight-knit community of cowboys and their families, she suspected news traveled fast. Just because she hadn't come out of the basement for longer than ten minutes didn't mean no one knew she was there.

"Oh, I don't think—"

"It's the best spring activity," another woman said.

"I go every year," someone else chimed in.

"You simply have to go," Tess said. "We plant them in

May and harvest them in August. It's a family tradition of ours that made it through the marriage."

Molly didn't know what that meant, but all the women were looking at her like she should be dying to plant some strawberries. She glanced at Emmett but he was absolutely no help. Typical.

"When is it?" she asked, hoping she'd be working. Or dead. Then she wouldn't have to go.

"This Saturday." Tess beamed at her. "I have a two for one coupon."

"I'm using that," Emmett finally piped up.

"Oh, really?" Tess rounded on Emmett faster than anything Molly had ever seen. "Who are you taking?"

"Yeah," Megan said. "Last time we talked, you said you weren't interested in women."

Molly sipped her coffee, her ears on high alert. Why would a man like Emmett—smart, resourceful, handsome—choose to be single? She nearly choked again when she thought of the three positive attributes she'd given him. In the end, she mentally shrugged. He was smart, he was resourceful, and she couldn't deny his handsomeness. Yes, there was definitely a woman out there who would love to fall into those cloudy, gray eyes and swim around for a while.

Molly found herself doing so now, while everyone else was staring at Emmett too.

"I'm not," he said.

"You can't have the coupon if you're not taking someone," Tess said.

"I think Grant would like to go."

"Mm, no," Tess said. "You cowboys can pay for yourselves. You can only have the coupon if you take a date."

"Fine." Emmett placed his coffee mug in the sink, causing a riot of panic to spike in Molly's chest. She was nowhere near finished with her coffee, but she couldn't be left alone here with all these women.

"What about Molly?" Tess asked next, and Megan the Traitor jumped right on the bandwagon.

"Oh, that's a good idea." She looked at Molly and then Emmett. "She's new to town, Emmett. You could show her around."

"Why don't *you* show her around?" he growled. "I already gave her a tour of the ranch."

"See? You're the best tour guide." Tess beamed at him, and Molly thought he'd shoot lasers from his eyes. They had a special relationship that intrigued Molly, and she wanted to know more about it.

"I'll go," she said. "I mean, I like strawberries, I guess." What's more, she really didn't want to spend another weekend trapped in the basement by herself. All she'd do is obsess over her father's health and if she should jump into her truck and head east.

Emmett stared openly at her, his eyes a bit wider than normal. "You'll go?"

"As long as it's not a date. I'll even pay for you."

Stunned silence drifted through the room like no one had ever suggested such a thing. Then the women twittered, and Tess sidled up to Molly. "Oh, honey, let him pay for you."

She glanced at the woman and found fondness in her

expression as she gazed at Emmett. "He needs to get out. Thanks for saying you'll go."

With that, the ranch wives left the kitchen almost as fast as they'd come. Molly stood there, wondering if she'd just been the butt of some joke, caught on candid camera, or something else equally embarrassing.

Emmett put his hand on her elbow and said, "Can I talk to you for a sec?" before towing her out of the kitchen and into the backyard.

## Chapter 5

Pure humiliation pulled through Emmett. He couldn't believe Megan and Tess—the masterminds behind getting him to go out with someone. And not just someone—Molly.... He couldn't even remember the woman's last name! That was how little he cared about getting to know her.

Yet something had awakened inside him when he'd caught her bent over her phone, weeping. Call him sentimental, or soft-hearted, or romantic, but he'd felt sorry for her. He'd wanted to help, and holding her hand felt as natural as being in the saddle.

Molly had let him too, which had surprised him at the same time it pleased him. She put on a good show of being a tough cowgirl, but he'd seen a softer side of her he *did* want to pursue.

"Can you let go of me?" she asked, the ice back in her tone.

He didn't. Instead, he slid his hand down her arm to her hand. He laced his fingers in hers and held on. Shock mixed with rage and streamed through Molly's eyes with the fierceness of a tornado.

Emmett hung on. "Look," he said, his voice getting stuck in the back of his throat, making the word sound husky and growly. "I'm with you. We can go together as long as this isn't counted as a date."

Everything about her softened, and Emmett wondered why she put on such a show. "I'll even pay for half of your ticket if this isn't counted as a date," she said.

He dropped her hand. "I'm that repulsive, huh?"

Molly blinked. "No," she said, though Emmett was sure she was about to say yes.

He grinned. "Good, because you're definitely not repulsive." When his brain caught up to what his mouth had said, he spun away from the cowgirl and strode toward the gate. He had to get away from her. Get away from her now.

Because she was making all the things he'd already chosen for his life muddled. Maybe he did want a girlfriend. Maybe he could find a woman to settle down with. Maybe, maybe, maybe. Emmett thought he'd lose his mind, and it wasn't even lunchtime yet.

*You've a long way to go*, he told himself as he marched back to the horse barn, Molly right beside him. He waved her into the barn first, and then he pressed his eyes closed and uttered a simple prayer. *Guide me.*

---

SATURDAY ARRIVED IN A WINDY, whirly mess. Emmett's first thought was that he could easily get out of going to the strawberry planting that morning. The event might even be cancelled. Hope ballooned in his chest as he put together a western omelet for breakfast and opened a can of cat food for his calico tabby cat.

"Tigress," he called, adding a whistle to his statement. The cat emerged from the bedroom, where she'd been curled up beside him all night. He hadn't been lying when he'd told Molly part of his heart belonged to this feline.

She purred as she rubbed against his ankles, and he bent down to give her a proper pat. "Time to eat." He lifted her onto the counter where her bowl sat and they ate breakfast together.

He'd made it through the week with Molly at his side. She didn't try to argue with him again, and she didn't correct him. He took her through how he'd start a horse, and last night, Landon had said he'd be taking Molly and Emmett to Green River to look at potential new steeds to start.

Since then his phone had been going off non-stop. Why he'd decided to give his phone number to Molly, he wasn't sure.

"Sure you are," he muttered as his phone chimed for the first time that morning. He was sure it wouldn't be the last. He'd given his number to Molly and told her to call anytime, day or night, when he'd caught her weeping in the barn on Wednesday. Apparently her father had been cleared to go home though he was still quite ill and had entered the first stages of kidney failure.

His heart had gone out to her, and he'd sat next to her, his back pressing into the stall door until she'd quieted. She'd held his hand, and Emmett admitted that it felt nice to be connected to someone in such an intimate way.

Which was why he reached for his phone and read her message. *We really don't have to go today.*

And why he sent back, *I want to go today.*

*It's not a date.*

*What if I said I wanted it to be?* Emmett stared at the words, his tongue thick in his mouth and his omelet forgotten. He was sure Molly would freak out and refuse to come upstairs if he sent it. No, he needed to handle her the way he would one of his most skittish horses.

So he thumbed off the message that revealed how he really felt and typed *We should still go. It'll be fun.*

Her response came several minutes later, after Emmett had scraped his uneaten cold eggs into the trash and put out water for Tigress. *Can I come over for a few minutes?*

*I have a cat.*

*We can sit on your front porch.*

*Whatever you want, sweetheart.* He did take a chance and send that one, and then he shut Tigress in his bedroom and stepped onto the porch, keeping all her dander and fur and other allergy-causing issues inside the cabin.

Molly showed up a few minutes later, and Emmett's mouth turned dry as he watched her cross the lane and come toward his cabin. She wore khaki capris that showed off the muscles in her legs and a frilly red top the color of strawberries. He reminded himself to breathe when he saw the strappy sandals and her bright red toenails.

He didn't think redheads actually wore red, but Molly made the color look amazing. She sat herself next to him and wrapped her arms around her knees as she pulled them to her chest. It was these vulnerable moments Emmett liked best about her. He thought the other, tough woman was an act. Someone she pretended to be. Someone she thought she needed to be for some reason.

"Is it a good morning?" he asked.

She shot him a quick smile and said, "Yeah." She released one of her arms and rested her hand on his knee. His pulse jumped and his blood turned to liquid fire and he reached for her fingers and held them lightly in his.

"Tell me what's goin' on," he said.

She scooted a little closer and rested her head on his shoulder. "You have a...magical way...." she whispered. "I can't explain it, but you...."

He lifted her wrist to his lips, causing her to suck in a breath and hold it. Emmett's mouth curved up and he lowered his hand and he breathed with Molly.

"Are you sayin' you don't hate me?" he asked, daring to break this peaceful silence.

"No," she said, her breath heating his shoulder through his shirt. "I don't hate you."

Emmett's mind raced and he employed his neutral voice when he asked, "Are you sayin' you like me?"

She nudged him with her knees. "I'm still trying to decide."

"Is that why you don't want to go to the strawberry fields with me today?"

"I'm—Do you really think Landon is going to have me start training a horse right away?"

Emmett's defenses flew back into position. "No, Molly," he said just as he had in his texts to her last night. "I don't think he'll have you start for a few months. I think he'll get us a horse we can take through the process together." He squeezed her hand and let go, especially when the front door of the cabin next door opened. He shot to his feet, practically throwing Molly away from him when Tess exited.

She didn't even glance in their direction, thankfully, but Molly got the message. What message that was, Emmett wasn't entirely sure, but by the time he turned to check on her she had already crossed his lawn.

No goodbye, no nothing. He sighed and pulled out his phone to text her. But an apology seemed stupid on the screen, and he ended up going back into his cabin without sending her anything.

He leaned against the closed door, wondering if she could let down her guard long enough for him to let down his. Why did he care if Tess saw them holding hands? Fear bolted straight through his heart. He knew what holding hands led to, and it started with a *g*– and ended with –*irlfriend*.

And girlfriends became fiancés, and fiancés became wives, and wives became ex-wives. He took a deep breath and steeled himself against the beauty of vulnerability of Molly Brady. He reminded himself of the mother he hadn't seen in twenty years, and the father who'd tried to find a replacement for her and had failed two more times.

Emmett didn't need that drama in his life. No sirree. Dating, and women, and marriage simply weren't for him.

Which made Molly's next text doubly upsetting.

*Next time we'll have to sit on your back porch. Or inside. I might be able to brave the cat.*

He stared at the phone, trying to decipher the message. He felt like he needed a translator, a key to crack the code, in order to speak with women. He had no idea how to respond, and feared that if he didn't get it right, a bomb might go off.

An hour later, he opened the door to Michael's knock, who asked, "Are you riding with us?"

Emmett had always gone down the canyon to the strawberry fields with Walker and Tess and their boys. Today, though, he glanced across the street to the homestead. "I think I'm gonna go with Molly." He smiled at the boy who ran back to Walker's big black truck and climbed in the back.

Tess met his eye and lifted her hand, and from this distance, Emmett couldn't decide if she was smirking at him or wishing him well. *Probably both*, he thought as he crossed the street and knocked on the front door.

Only moments later, Molly opened it. "Oh, hello."

"It's time to go," he said. "Do you want to drive, or should I?"

She snatched her keys off the front table as if she alone owned the homestead, and said, "I will," before marching past him like she'd rather swim with sharks with an open wound than allow him to drive her anywhere.

Emmett sighed, annoyed with himself for being half-amused by her behavior, and followed her down the sidewalk.

---

EMMETT'S STOMACH twisted as she curved down the roads and entered the town. He needed to just tell Molly why he held women at arm's length—why he'd dropped her hand so abruptly that morning.

She seemed content behind the wheel, and she eased to a stop at the junction of Main Street. "Which way do I go?"

"Left," he said. "The strawberry fields are up the road to the north about five minutes." Emmett swallowed and looked out the window the way he'd been doing for the past fifteen minutes. "Stay on this street and head out of town," he added once she turned.

They passed the bakery, the church, and continued down the main shopping district in town. "Look," he said as she left town. "I—" He exhaled. "I've—wow, this is harder than I thought it would be."

She cut him a glance out of the corner of her eye. "Do you have a secret family in Napa Valley or something? A wife hidden away? Two cute little boys with your pretty eyes?"

Emmett started shaking his head before she finished talking. "No, I—you think my eyes are pretty?" He was glad she'd chosen to drive, because then he could study her.

She lifted one slim shoulder, disrupting that silky blouse. "You know they are."

"I do?"

"Please." She gave him a death glare. "I know all about handsome men like you. I wasn't the first woman you tried to pick up at that country line dance."

"I—" Emmett sputtered at the ridiculousness of her statement. "I wasn't picking you up. I don't do that. I just —I like to dance with someone."

"It's line dancing," she said.

"Yeah, and I like the social aspect of it. I have never, never picked someone up." He let the disgust in his voice permeate his voice. "I go to church every week, I'll have you know."

"You do?"

"Yeah. Do you?"

"Maybe not every week." She squirmed in her seat, something he hadn't seen her do in the horse arena while on Hurricane. She was supremely confident there, and now she wasn't.

"So I talked to you at a dance. You were rude," he said, his original topic of conversation fading.

"I was not."

He chuckled. "Molly, I don't even think you realize how cold you are."

Her fingers clenched on the wheel and an angry flush rushed up her neck.

"Look, that's not what I was trying to say. No, I don't have a secret wife or family or any cute boys with my *pretty eyes* hidden away somewhere."

"Then anything you say now is easy."

Emmett kicked a grin in her direction, but she didn't see him. "Is this it?"

He focused on the road and said, "Yes, turn left here. The strawberry fields are up on the right." He took a deep breath. "I haven't dated in a while, because I'm honestly not interested in getting married."

She pulled into the dirt parking lot and found a space. She put the truck in park and turned the ignition off before she twisted toward him and met his eyes. "You're not?"

"My dad, well, let's just say that all the men in my family have been divorced, some more than once. My mom left us when I was twelve, and I just don't need any of that in my life." He sighed. "I have my horses, and my cat, and well, I always thought that would be enough."

Molly took a few minutes to absorb his words, something he appreciated. "I'm sorry about your mom."

"Thank you," he said, noticing the steady stream of people heading down the path and into the fields. "Should we go?"

"Yeah. No." She unbuckled her seat belt and paused. "You said you *thought* that would be enough. Do you still feel like that?" She squinted at him, something he noticed her doing often. He wondered if she needed glasses or she was fine-tuning her superhero sight.

He shook his head. "I don't know. Kinda like how you're trying to decide if you like me. I'm trying to decide if I could do any better than my dad and brothers. I guess I'm trying to figure out if dating you is worth potentially getting my heart stomped on."

She flinched, and a hard edge entered her eyes. "I'm probably not." She got out of the truck and Emmett joined her. She put her hand in his and added, "But Emmett, look around you. There are four cowboys living right next door to you who've taken the risk. Who're happy with their choice. None of the ranch wives are running away. No divorces there."

Emmett considered her words, thought through his friends on the ranch. "April came to Brush Creek pregnant. Their baby isn't Ted's. I mean, it is, because he adopted the baby. But yeah."

"And they're happy now. Maybe you just need to adjust who you're looking at for examples. That's all I'm saying." They arrived at the ticket booth, and Emmett presented his coupon and paid for their entrance to the fields.

Once through the gate, Emmett distracted himself from Molly's very wise words with fertilizer, dirt, and strawberry plants. If he didn't, he might actually take her advice and get out of his own way when it came to women.

And not just any woman. Molly.

# Chapter 6

Molly enjoyed the hours she spent at the strawberry fields with Emmett. Sure, he stared at her when he thought she wasn't looking. For anyone else, she'd raise her eyes to theirs and cock her eyebrows, maybe even stalk over to them and demand, "What?"

But she'd appreciated Emmett's honesty with her. She hated to admit it, but she'd misjudged him the first time they'd met. And she'd probably been rude. She'd only been at the ranch for a week, and she could feel the love the people and families there had for each other. One only needed to eat a single meal with them to know, and she wondered how far gone Emmett must be for him to miss it.

She'd had an emotional week, and working with earth and plants calmed her. It had been stressful learning a new job, dealing with new co-workers, learning about her father's continued poor health. Emmett had been there every step of the way, reassuring her, comforting her, being kind to her. It had been nice to have someone. And not just someone. Someone she wasn't constantly second-guessing, wondering why he was being nice to her, what he'd want from her later.

So it was that she touched his back as she passed him to put her fledgling plant in the row next to the one he was currently embedding in the dirt. He glanced at her, and something hot passed between them.

He tapped her shoulder and asked her if she wanted some water, and when he brought it back, he lingered in her personal space. She liked the dance. The little touches. The exchanged glances.

Molly wasn't sure she could allow more, but for now, she was keeping her options open. She knew that if these easy flirtations turned into something more serious, she'd have to tell Emmett about her stalker, as well as her nonexistent maternal instincts.

"Look at you two."

Molly glanced up at Tess, who stood with a tall cowboy and two boys who couldn't be more different. She straightened and smiled. "Hey, Tess. Are you guys done?"

Emmett joined her and knocked knuckles with the two boys. He seemed so natural with kids, and Molly marveled at his ability to do so.

"Yeah, we just finished. Do you guys want to go to lunch together?" Tess glanced at her husband, whose name Molly thought was Walker. "We'll wait for you. Looks like you're almost done."

Emmett shifted closer to Molly, clearly deferring to her. His fingers brushed hers and disappeared. She looked at Emmett and back to the family standing before her. "I think Emmett was going to take me to Beaverton for lunch." She locked eyes with him, finding the surprise there. "Right?"

"Sure, yeah." He brushed his hands on his jeans and seemed fascinated by the ground. "Molly loves Chinese food."

"No," Molly said quickly. "Remember how you said they have great onion rings at that drive-through?"

"No Chinese food?" Emmett studied her, and he sure wasn't good at keeping up a ruse.

She smiled and tucked her elbow into his arm. "I think we're just going to go to lunch by ourselves. Thanks, though."

Tess's sharp eyes didn't miss anything, and Molly found herself admiring the woman. "All right." She started down the path, and her boys went with her. She'd paced away several steps, and Emmett had retrieved another plant and moved down the row to the next spot, when Tess returned.

She looked right into Molly's eyes, hers dancing with light. "You like him, right?"

Molly barely knew Tess, but she said, "Yeah."

"Be careful with him." She glanced down the row and back to her family. "He's...new to this kind of stuff."

Molly wanted to tell Tess that so was she, that she hadn't dated anyone seriously until she was twenty-five, and then she'd had one boyfriend who'd turned psycho. But she simply said, "Okay," and let Tess go.

"What'd she say?" Emmett stood only a step behind her, and Molly followed his gaze as he watched Tess leave with her family.

"How well do you know her?"

He ran his hands from her bare shoulder to her wrist

and back. Molly had the dangerous inclination to close her eyes and sigh under the strength and warmth of his touch. Thankfully, she didn't let herself exhibit such revealing actions.

"Really well. She's like a mother figure for me."

"She can't be much older than you."

"She's not. She's had a rough life, and she's come through it. I look up to her, usually listen to her when she talks, that sort of thing." He glanced back the way Tess had gone. "Her first husband died at the company he owned, and not a year later she was diagnosed with breast cancer. She and Walker were married on the way to the hospital just before she got a mastectomy."

Molly's admiration for the woman went through the roof. "I can see why you like her. She just said I needed to be careful with you."

His light eyes darkened. "I disagree." He ducked his head and picked up another plant. "Come on. Let's finish, and then we'll have to drive around to find those onion rings." He gave her his classic arrogant smirk, but it was starting to grow on her, so the only emotion that tripped through her was delight that they'd get to spend some more time together.

―――

SHE POLISHED off the last onion ring at his insistence, the last hour in the restaurant one of the best in Molly's life. Well, maybe she'd put her championship wins above the lunch. At this point, it was a toss up as she'd left that life behind and was trying to carve out a new one.

*A new one with Emmett?*

The jury was still out.

And she didn't need their verdict right now anyway. She could hold his hand, and laugh with him, and ask him questions about training a horse from wild to champion without knowing how things would end with them.

She parked in front of his cabin instead of pulling around to the north end of the homestead, where she'd been parking in the RV bay.

"I have a cat," he reminded her. "Let me go shut her in the bedroom."

Molly let him leap from the truck and jog across the lawn. He didn't have to unlock the door, which fascinated her. She'd locked every door behind her for a solid year, and she still barricaded herself in her bedroom in the basement.

She told herself she didn't need to be afraid anymore, that Clay had no idea where she was and he wouldn't dare defy the restraining order anyway. If he did, he wouldn't be able to compete in the rodeo, and she knew that was more important to him than she was.

Emmett came back out to the porch, and Molly got out of her truck. He received her straight into his arms, and she tipped her face back to look into his. If he would just dip his mouth down, he could kiss her.

Her heart started to race like she'd just given her horse the signal to start a barrel run. His shoulders beneath her fingers felt firm and fantastic, and she felt flirty and fun for the first time in a long time.

"It was a great day, wasn't it?" she asked.

"We haven't had ice cream yet." He grinned wickedly and led her into his cabin. The clicking of the door behind her almost made Molly bolt, but she reminded herself that Emmett wasn't Clay. That she *wanted* to be here with him.

The back of her throat started to itch, but she ignored it. "We just finished eating," she said as she glanced around. The cabin was nice—nicer than anything she'd lived in since graduating high school. Hardwood floors and slate gray walls with wood accents and exposed beams. The kitchen had quartz countertops, tile, and stainless steel appliances—and Emmett standing at the freezer.

"And the day's far from over," he said, closing the freezer. "So maybe...I don't know. You want to take a ride and then have ice cream?"

She rubbed her eyes. "Sure. Or we can just watch a movie. Take an afternoon nap."

He glanced at the couch in his living room and swiped his cowboy hat off to scrub the curly hair on the back of his head. Molly smiled at the nervous gesture. "Let me guess. You haven't had a woman in your cabin in a long time."

"You could've just stopped at I haven't had a woman in my cabin." He met her eyes, worry in his. "Ever."

"So I'm the first?" She strutted toward him, adding a little extra swing to her hips. He licked his lips as she advanced, and she was glad to know she wasn't the only one thinking about kissing.

"The very first. I haven't dated since I moved here."

"I bet the available ladies in town are disappointed by that." She paused just outside his personal bubble, her own nerves starting a coup inside her chest.

"I wouldn't know." He glanced at the back door. "I'll grab you some Benadryl and we can sit on the back porch.

It won't be in the shade, but we can move the chairs under the trees if you want."

"I don't need—"

"Your eyes are turning red, and your whole face is puffing up." He gave her that self-assured grin and went into the bathroom while she escaped all things cat and grabbed one of the camp chairs on the back porch and took it to the stand of trees bordering his lawn before the hay fields took over.

He joined her a minute or two later, with two bottles of water and two pills for her. He didn't sit in the camp chair he'd brought, but continued to a tree trunk and leaned against it. The sunlight haloed him, and his silhouette with that cowboy hat was one of the sexiest things Molly had ever seen.

She sucked in a breath and made her decision. She wanted to let him know she liked him. So she pushed herself up and joined him at the tree line. "Emmett?"

"Hmm?" He didn't look at her but continued to gaze at the breathtaking horizon.

"I've decided that I like you."

That got his attention and he turned his whole body toward her. "Is that right?" The swagger he'd possessed the first night she'd blown him off presented itself, and she swatted his chest.

"You don't have to be so proud of yourself."

"I'm not." He drew her into his arms and ducked his head so his words tickled her ear when he said, "I'm nervous."

She sucked in her response when his lips lightly touched the top of her earlobe, and then nipped the bottom of it.

Unconsciously, she clung to him, sure she'd fall without his support.

He placed a kiss on her neck, just below her ear, and she murmured, "You're missing."

"Missing what?" His husky voice held equal parts desire and apprehension.

"My mouth."

He pulled back and their eyes locked. "I've decided I like you too," he said, all the encouragement Molly needed.

She stretched up and closed the distance between her mouth and his. While she hadn't had much experience in the kissing department, the way he explored without demanding, used the right amount of pressure to indicate his feelings, and held her close with those large hands made for an experience she wouldn't soon forget.

# Chapter 7

If Emmett had known how exhilarating kissing a woman he liked could be, he might have made more of an effort to overcome his familial issues. As it was, he didn't have a lot of practice with kissing women, but the way Molly sighed against his lips and kissed him back eagerly, he figured he was doing something right.

After what felt like a long time, she broke their connection and giggled as she rested her forehead against his collarbone. Emmett held her in his arms and gazed into the distance, wondering what he'd just gotten himself into.

His toes tingled and he swallowed hard, the comforting feeling of Molly in his arms wonderful and vibrant. "So, napping or horseback riding?" he asked. He wasn't sure he could contain himself behind walls on such a gorgeous afternoon, and a skiff of nerves accompanied the thought of hanging out in his boss's basement. But his house was obviously out, as Tigress caused a real problem for Molly.

"Horseback riding," she said. "And then I think you promised me ice cream."

Emmett grinned at her, held her hand in his as they crossed the lawn, the street, and through the ranch to the barn. "You want to take Beauty today?"

She paused, turning her hazel eyes to his. "You're going to let me ride your treasured horse?"

Emmett grunted. "Hurricane misses me." He stopped outside the horse's stall. "Don't you, boy?"

Molly laughed and continued to Beauty, toward whom Emmett did shoot a longing glance. He did love Beauty, but she'd have to get used to a woman on her back soon enough. Might as well be Molly.

With the horses saddled and their cowboy hats in place, Emmett led Molly north and west of the ranch along a dirt road that eventually ended in a much narrower trail.

"How's your father?" he asked as he eased ahead of her.

"Doing a lot better. I still worry about him, though."

"Of course." Emmett steered Hurricane down a slight incline that would take them to the stream. At this point in the spring, it would be rushing, full of water from the melted snow off the mountain. By the end of the summer, the water barely trickled through the riverbed.

"Tell me about your family."

And so they swapped stories of their families, their childhoods, and their time in the rodeo. Emmett hadn't thought conversing with a woman could be as pleasurable as it was with Molly, and by the time they arrived at the stream, he wanted to kiss her again. Badly.

He dismounted and let Hurricane drink, his thoughts swimming far away and then surfing back. Molly stepped to his side and he automatically drew her hand into his, wanting to be close to her, needed to be grounded by human touch.

"I don't think I realized how lonely I was," he murmured.

Molly squeezed his fingers. "Surrounded by people but always alone."

He looked at her, and she lifted one shoulder in a sexy shrug. "I've been there. Still am, most days."

Emmett leaned over and touched his lips to hers, barely a union but enough to send fireworks through his system. When he refocused on the stream, the colors seemed brighter. The sun warmer. The silence more comforting. With Molly, everything was simply better, and he sighed with happiness.

---

THE FOLLOWING DAY, Emmett sat in his truck, waiting for Molly to come out of the homestead. While she'd admitted that she hadn't been to church in a while, she was also willing to go with him.

Landon and Megan pulled out in their minivan, and Emmett waved and watched as they disappeared down the lane. With only twenty minutes until the sermon started, Molly jogged through the front door. "I'm so sorry," she said as she climbed in the truck. She scooted all the way over next to him and planted a kiss on his cheek. "I sort of lost track of time."

"What were you doin' in there?" he asked as he put the truck in gear. She wore a little black dress that had

Emmett's heart pumping hard, and bright yellow heels that made him chuckle. "Nice shoes."

"I was trying to tame my curls." She reached up and pulled her fingers through her hair. "I'm out of this curl cream I use, and it's a real problem."

He glanced at her hair and thought it looked just fine. "You should talk to Tess," he said. "She's a hairdresser, and can probably get you something."

"The technical term is stylist." Molly laughed and put her hand on his leg. Emmett sucked in a breath, fire exploding up and down from the origin of her touch.

"All right," he said, his voice only slightly scratchy. "She's a *stylist*."

Molly fidgeted next to him as he drove down the canyon. He parked and secured her hand in his as he strode toward the church. The doors were already closed, which meant the meeting had started. Anxiety wound through him. Now they'd have to walk in late, an open invitation for everyone to stare at them.

Emmett thought hard about holding Molly's hand in front of the whole blasted town. In front of Landon and Megan, Walker and Tess, everyone at the ranch. His stomach twisted, but he held tight to Molly's fingers and opened the door.

Sure enough, the organ was playing and the choir was singing, but at least the preacher hadn't started yet. He crossed the foyer and paused in the doorway, finding an open bench halfway down on the left easily enough. He towed Molly along beside him and slid into the seat, his heart pounding, pounding, pounding.

Ted and April sat on the back row. Surely they'd seen

him. He wondered how long it would take the bronc rider to message him and say something. Blake and Erin sat there too, with all of her kids, and Emmett resisted the urge to turn and see if they were staring. It felt like everyone was staring.

His phone buzzed, dread threaded through him. He pulled it from his pocket and checked it anyway, finding a message of *Are you holding that woman's hand?* from Ted.

Before Emmett could even roll his eyes, a new text arrived from Tess. *How was your date yesterday?*

*And then I'm so glad you brought her to church with you! You two are so cute.*

Emmett rolled his eyes and silenced his phone completely, shoving it in his back pocket with a little too much force.

The choir had finished and the preacher stood at the pulpit. "Let's think about the Lord's sacrifice for us today," he said, and Emmett was instantly swept away by Pastor Peters' calm voice and obvious passion for God. A rush of gratitude filled him, not only for the Savior's love and sacrifice, but for the preacher and the people in this town.

The meeting ended, but Molly didn't get up. She continued to stare toward the front of the chapel until Emmett said, "You okay?"

"Do you believe everything he just said?" she asked without looking away from where Pastor Peters stood, talking to a couple of older ladies who sat in Widow Row—the front row of the chapel.

"Yes," Emmett said. "Do you?"

She swung her gaze toward him then, and he found tears in the corners of her eyes. "I want to talk to him." She stood and strode faster than Emmett thought possible in those yellow pinpoint heels toward the pulpit. Emmett scurried after her, unsure if this was proper protocol or not. The pastor often made his way to the doors and spoke with people there.

Molly waited until he finished with the widows, then she said, "Hello, Pastor. I'm Molly Brady. I'm new in town."

The preacher glanced at Emmett and back to Molly with a warm smile. "Welcome. How are you liking Brush Creek?"

"It's great. Fine." Molly wrung her hands together. "I just wanted to ask, I mean—Do you really think the Lord suffered for all our sins?"

Pastor Peters nodded, the intensity in his eyes sharpening again. "I don't just think it. I don't just believe it. I *know* it."

Emmett inched next to Molly and slipped his arm around her waist. She sagged into him, openly weeping now. "What if you've made some big mistakes?"

Alarms sounded in Emmett's head. What kind of mistakes could Molly have possibly made?

"I don't believe anyone has made a mistake they can't come back from," Pastor Peters said. "The Lord always wants you to return to Him."

Molly nodded, met Emmett's eye, and then turned and walked out. Emmett wasn't quite sure what to make of her behavior. Molly seemed so put together, despite her opinion that her hair didn't look right today. The fact was, Molly was the type of woman who always had everything lined up, all things in their place. Emmett had known lots of women like her—barrel racers had specific personalities.

"Thanks, Pastor." Emmett flashed a tight smile at the man still standing there and moved up the aisle as well. He didn't know what mistakes Molly had made, or how serious they were, but with every step he took he knew he wanted to be there to find out. Be there to support her. Be there when she fell apart so he could put her back together again.

He paused on the steps just outside the door, looking for her. She waited with her back to the chapel, the almost-summer breeze playing with her skirt, leaning against a tree.

He'd taken one step when Ted said, "So Emmett's got himself a girlfriend." Emmett moaned and turned back to his friends.

"Ted, come on. We're not fourteen."

But Ted grinned like he'd just won the lottery, and Emmett cast a longing glance at Molly.

## Chapter 8

Molly had gotten the tears to stop. Thankfully. She watched the water in the stream bordering the park swirl by, taking with it leaves, bits of debris, and small sticks. She wished she could jump into the water and have it carry her along without a care in the world.

But she couldn't. She'd been truthful when she'd told Emmett she hadn't been to church in a while. Her rodeo schedule didn't allow much time for worship, and Molly realized now how much she'd missed it. The all-encompassing peace, the way everything around her stilled, how her normal worries and cares faded into silence as she listened to the sermon.

She hadn't made any horrible, awful mistakes—at least that she knew of. But she found it miraculous that the Savior could take on the sins of those who had. Her thoughts had centered on Clay during most of the sermon, and she'd felt an overwhelming instinct that he'd been forgiven for what he'd done to her.

Not only that, she'd also felt like she now needed to forgive him too. She closed her eyes for the tenth time in as many minutes and prayed. *How do I do that? How can I forgive him for making my life a living nightmare for a whole year?*

She didn't have the answer. And she didn't have the forgiveness in her heart, which made tears prick her eyes again. Was she as bad as him, withholding her forgiveness?

Emmett finally joined her, standing nearby but not touching her. "Hey."

She stepped into his embrace and pressed her cheek to his shoulder.

His hands moved up and down her back, a welcome comfort when she felt so restless. "You okay?"

"Yes."

He sighed and she matched her breathing to his. "You'll probably never come to church with me again."

All at once, Molly had the answer to her prayers. She didn't know how she could forgive Clay right now, but if she kept coming to church, she'd find the answers she needed.

"No, I want to come every week," she said.

Emmett leaned back and looked at her. "Yeah?"

She smiled and though her face felt too hot and she was sure looked blotchy, she tipped up and kissed him quick. "Yeah."

---

A COUPLE of weeks passed with life as usual on the ranch, and at home. She called her mom every few days, but her father's health hadn't improved or declined. Something to be grateful for, she supposed.

She continued to work with Hurricane on tighter turns, and Emmett had just advanced them to full runs when Landon showed up one Friday morning.

"I got in at an auction happening tomorrow."

"Where?" Emmett asked.

"Cheyenne."

Emmett groaned, but Molly didn't know why. She'd been to Cheyenne lots of times, and it was a nice place. Well, nice enough.

Landon lifted his foot and rested it on the bottom rung of the fence separating the walkway surrounding the indoor arena from the practice area. "I know."

Emmett glared and turned back to Beauty, pretending to inspect one of her feet, though Molly had seen him do that exact check only ten minutes ago. "What's our budget?"

"I'm comin' with you."

"Oh yeah?" Emmett straightened, the surprise on his face saying that Landon didn't make these trips often.

"Yeah." He glanced over his shoulder and even Molly could tell he was trying for nonchalance. "I think it'll be nice to get away for a couple of days."

"How long does an auction last?" Molly asked.

"Just a couple of hours." Landon gave her a friendly smile.

"Then why do we stay for a couple of days?" She switched her gaze back and forth between the two cowboys. She couldn't believe how far she'd come in only a month.

Being in the same space as cowboys used to make her want to chew off her own arm just to get away.

But she liked these men. Her gaze landed on Emmett, and she admitted to herself that she liked him a lot.

"We always meet with the breeder after the purchase," Emmett said. "Then Landon likes to check out a couple of places in Cheyenne for supplies, and then he meets up with some old friends. So we stay the night."

"Is that a problem?" Landon asked.

"I thought Blake was going to start on the cabin tomorrow," Molly said. "I was hoping to be here to help, but if he won't mind...."

"He won't mind," Landon said. "Blake prefers to work alone anyway."

Molly thought that might be code for, "So leave him alone and just let him build the cabin," but she didn't quite know Landon well enough to know for sure.

"Sounds great," she said, though everything about Emmett said it wasn't. Landon nodded once and left the indoor facility.

"Why do you meet with the breeder?" Molly asked once he'd gone.

"Landon's fussy, that's why."

"Yeah, but really why?"

"He has this list of questions. Stuff about growth rates, any illnesses in infancy, that kind of stuff."

"Seems smart."

Emmett's bad mood evaporated as he gazed at her. "You would think so."

"Ha ha." She turned away from him and mounted her

horse. "Did you see the way he pulled across the last barrel? Why's he doing that?" Molly had gained new respect for Emmett and others who trained the horses she rode to victory. It wasn't an easy or a fast process, and she hadn't known all of what went into making her horse do what he did during a run.

Emmett started talking, and Molly tried to absorb all she could. "Oh, and I hate Cheyenne, because it's a five hour drive, and Landon always tries to set me up with one of his best friends who used to ride."

Molly blinked at him. "You've been off the circuit for a while if five hours is a long drive." She directed her horse over to where Emmett stood and leaned down to kiss him. "And you won't have to worry about that friend this time. Just send her in my direction. I'll tell her what's what."

Emmett chuckled. "I think I'd really like to see that." He backed up a step and looked at her with a serious edge in his eye. "And I think I'd like to know what's what too."

"You don't know?" She enjoyed flirting with him, and though she hadn't done much of it in her life, she thought she was really good at pushing his buttons.

"Enlighten me." He swung onto his horse too, grace and power combined into one lean body.

Molly blushed, because while she knew how she felt about Emmett and how it would likely surface if another pretty barrel racer tried to hit on him, she thought it would sound stupid said out loud.

"You know," she said, trotting her horse a few feet from him.

He swung in front of her. "Remember how you were the first woman to enter my cabin? Trust me when I say I don't know."

"Well, you'll have to figure it out then." She gave him a coy smile and took Hurricane down to the end of the alley for another run.

Later that night, she ascended the steps to Megan's kitchen, where a couple of ladies—April and Renee—had already arrived. Renee stirred something on the stove that smelled cheesy and spicy at the same time while April opened four bags of chips.

"Molly, there you are." Megan barely glanced at her as she carefully spread chocolate frosting on an already iced cake. "Can you run out to the third garage and grab the sodas from the extra fridge?"

"Sure." She swiped her forefinger through the frosting, and Megan shrieked. Molly laughed. "Oh, come on. We all know Tess is going to win again." She danced away from Megan's wounded look, still chuckling. She'd only been to two other nights like this one, but she'd really enjoyed them. For the first time in her life, she had actual girlfriends—and not ones she was secretly, and not-so-secretly, hoping to beat in the next weekend's rodeo.

Molly had hung on the fringes at the first girl's night-slash-chocolate party. She hadn't made anything sweet or savory to bring to that shindig, and she'd felt guilty about eating everyone else's. At least until Tess had brought her a piece of Oreo pie and a fork and said she'd force-feed it to Molly if she had to.

Tess was the best baker in town, evidenced by that fact that the very women trying to beat her with their own homemade treats each week continued to vote for her.

Molly collected the twelve-pack of diet cola and the twelve-pack of grape soda—her favorite—and returned to the kitchen. Tess had obviously just arrived because she still had her brownie pan in one hand, with a container of ice cream in the other.

"We have a chance tonight, ladies!" April called. "Tess only brought brownies."

"Ah," Tess said with a smile and a flourish as she set her pan on the counter. "These are the ultimate fudgy brownies, and homemade mocha ice cream." She plunked the container next to the brownies, a satisfied—and probably justified—smirk on her face.

Molly crossed into the kitchen and put the sodas on the end of the counter near the snacks. Then she removed the top of the ice cream container and took a taste of that too. "She's winning," she said upon swallowing. She had no doubt that her fudgy brownies would be fantastically moist and deliciously chewy, and paired with that coffee ice cream?

"She's definitely winning."

"You haven't even tasted my Nutella dream cake," Renee protested, twisting from the stove.

"Or my hot chocolate mint whoopee pies." Megan looked completely betrayed, and Molly held up her hands in surrender.

"We'll try them all before we decide," Tess said. She bumped her hip into Molly's. "But I'm totally winning."

Chatter filled the house, and Molly marveled at it. She hadn't felt so at home, well, since she'd left Nebraska at age eighteen. She hadn't thought she could find friendship and camaraderie outside of her parents, and the rodeo circuit hadn't provided a safe haven for her, especially after she started winning.

She didn't have to have her hair perfectly styled for them to like her. She wasn't wearing makeup, and no one noticed. They didn't care that she'd won six national championships. If she cried, they'd rush to put their arms around her, not whisper behind her back and be glad that there were some things that didn't go her way.

"Let's eat," Megan announced, setting a stack of paper plates next to the steaming pot of queso con chili and the mini Swedish meatballs. Molly didn't hesitate this time but loaded her plate with one of everything on the counter, including the four rich, chocolate desserts. She hadn't brought anything this time either, and she only felt a twinge of guilt. She'd reasoned that no one would want anything she tried to make anyway.

They gathered in the living room, and Megan had barely eaten one chip before she said, "So, I hear you're going to Cheyenne with Emmett tomorrow." She accompanied the statement with a sly look and delicately placed another dipped chip in her mouth.

Silence fell in the house, as if someone had pushed mute on the conversation. Molly glanced at Megan, and then Tess. For some reason, she cared what the blonde-haired woman thought about her, and her relationship with Emmett.

Molly swallowed her meatball and shrugged. "Yeah, there's an auction, and Landon wants a new horse. He's going too."

"Yeah, to chaperone," Megan said in a sing-song voice.

Molly scoffed. "Nothing to chaperone. Emmett and I work together all day, and we don't have a babysitter."

"Which is why I got this." Tess swiped a few times on

her phone and then turned the screen so everyone could see. Molly snatched it before anyone else could, horrified by the picture of her and Emmett in a passionate embrace.

"When did you take this?"

"Yesterday afternoon, while you were 'working'." Tess's pealing laughter filled the house. "Oh, go on, Molly. Don't be embarrassed. I think it's sweet. You know Emmett hasn't dated in years. You've been very good for him."

Molly wanted to say that he'd been very good for her, but she simply smiled, handed the phone back to Tess, and put another delectable bite of Renee's Nutella dream cake in her mouth.

# Chapter 9

Emmett entered the outdoors while the sun still slept. Thankfully, he wasn't the only one as he found Landon leaning against the truck, the horse trailer already hitched up. "Seen Molly yet?"

"Yeah, she ran in to get her hat."

Emmett nodded, hoping he didn't seem too eager. He supposed a five-hour car ride with Molly would be better than without her. But half of him—all right, nearly all of him—wished he was going with her alone. They could attend the auction, get their horse, go to lunch, maybe find something to tour where he could hold her hand and find somewhere private to kiss her, and then drive home. Out before the sun came up; home after it went down.

"Things getting pretty serious with her?" Landon asked.

Emmett exhaled. "I honestly have no idea." He added a nervous chuckle. "How might I figure that out?"

Landon peered at him, and from the light on the porch, Emmett found amusement in his eyes. "You'll know,

Emmett. The important thing is not to do anything stupid until you know."

Emmett glanced back to his cabin, slightly annoyed. He didn't think he did stupid things, but he also knew stupidity was in the eye of the beholder.

Landon jangled the keys and Emmett looked at him, the noise further irritating him. "Well, Megan said she needs me this weekend." He sighed. "And I was sort of hoping for a little vacation."

Emmett didn't know what to say, but his ninja-like reflexes kicked in when Landon dropped the keys. "What?"

"Having a horse ranch, a wife, and three kids under age five is a little rough from time to time." He chuckled, but it sounded weary. He took a deep breath. "Anyway, the budget is one ten thousand. Do try to save me some money if you can."

Emmett stared at him, sure he'd heard his boss wrong. His heart tapped out a little dance in his chest at the prospect of this trip with Molly. "I'm sure we'll manage to get well below that."

"And since I'm not going, you and Molly can just come on home tonight."

"Will do."

Landon started to walk away, back toward the pool of light on the porch. "There's a Friesian in the auction I like. See what he's going for."

"You got it, boss." Emmett watched as Landon disappeared into the house and only about ten seconds later, Molly exited. Her step was hesitant as she approached, giving Emmett more time to drink in her long, jean-clad legs and her purple and black cowgirl shirt. She carried her hat, and her curls were immaculate.

"He's not coming?" She glanced back the way she'd come.

"Said Megan needed him this weekend." Emmett swept one arm around her and brought her into his chest. "How was your chocolate fest?" He tried to keep the jealousy from his voice, and he thought he did a decent job of it.

"Delicious." She giggled and stepped back. "But we need to take the kissing down while we work." She walked to the passenger door, Emmett following in her wake.

"Why?" He opened the door for her.

She turned in the opening, her eyes flashing with fire. "Tess took a picture of us kissing in the outdoor arena."

Emmett's chest seized. "She did?" He looked toward Cabin Row, but the horse trailer blocked the view.

"Hi-def," Molly said and climbed into the truck.

Emmett joined her, unsure of how he felt. He liked Molly a lot. If it were up to him, yeah, things would be getting serious. He had no idea how much time needed to pass before a relationship could be considered serious.

Blake and Erin had been dating for a year, and there were still two more months until their wedding. But Walker and Tess had only dated for a few months, and April and Ted had met, fallen in love, and tied the knot in only six months. Ted had wanted everything settled before the baby came, and he'd almost made it.

Justin had fallen in love with Renee in a summer as well. As Emmett thought through his friends on the ranch, he realized that none of them had needed much more than a few months to figure out how they felt.

And it had only been a month since Molly arrived at the ranch. Emmett settled into the drive, confident that he had a little more time to figure things out.

"Megan invited us to the Fourth of July pool party they're throwing in a couple of weeks."

Emmett said, "Sure. Sounds fun." He'd been to plenty of Megan's picnics, and he'd never regretted it. As the miles passed, he realized how right Molly had been. He did have some pretty good examples to look to, right here on the ranch. Couples who'd worked things out, moved past issues, had families.

An image of the mother he knew—the woman he'd known as a twelve-year-old boy—flashed through his mind. He wasn't sure what had been so terrible about her life that she'd had to leave it. Emmett assumed it must've been something awful, because she didn't even say goodbye.

He squirmed in his seat, desperate for a conversation to drive the negativity away. "Tell me about your first barrel racing horse," he said, because then Molly would talk and Emmett could get drunk on the pretty little sound of her voice.

---

"I can't believe you," Molly said, her voice incensed.

Emmett kept walking, his head held high. The woman had been a complete annoyance during the auction, pointing out all the things Emmett had already seen in the horses. Yes, she had a good eye. Yes, her concerns were legitimate.

But Landon wanted the Friesian, and maybe Emmett

*had* paid too much for him. Big deal. He was still under the ten thousand dollar ceiling.

"That's the horse I wanted," he said.

"The Appaloosa mix was a much better choice. He had Quarter Horse blood in him. The perfect combination for a barrel horse." She matched him stride for stride, her anger a scent on the air. "*And* he was cheaper."

"The Friesian will make a great barrel racing horse."

"That's not the point." Molly jumped in front of him, forcing him to stop. He glared at her, his blood running a little hotter when she gave his cutting look right back to him.

"What's the point then?" he asked.

"We came here to buy a horse *together*. A horse we're going to train *together*." Her chest heaved and she folded her arms across it, cocking that hip. "And you completely ignored me. Everything I said...." She shook her head, her eyes practically shooting fire at him. "How is that us working together?"

"Have you trained a horse from start to finish for barrel racing?"

Her jaw clenched.

"No, you haven't." Emmett softened his tone. "Maybe you'll just have to trust me." He tried to step past her—his client needed to be paid, and Emmett had his confidence built up to ask the questions Landon insisted upon.

But Molly would not be deterred. "You don't trust me. Why should I trust you?"

He fell back a step, stung. "I do too trust you." A new pinch started in his lungs, then his stomach, then the back of his throat, as if he'd swallowed a bumblebee and it was moving through his body, piercing him. "Why would you think otherwise?"

She lifted one hand and rubbed her forehead before settling her cowgirl hat back into place. "I mean—" When she looked at him again, he found more fear than fury.

Emmett waited with the same patience he used when trying to get Beauty to go down the alley. He folded his arms and shifted his weight, creating a mirror copy of Molly.

She swallowed. "Look, I couldn't trust very many people in the rodeo, cowboys least of all. This feels like I'm reliving all of that."

Emmett seized onto the words *cowboys least of all*. "What happened to you in the rodeo?" he asked, because something had happened.

"I don't really want to discuss it right now."

His heart thawed, and he took a step closer to her, leaning in. "So you'd rather just stomp after me, yelling?"

"I wasn't yelling."

"Why don't you trust cowboys?" Because while she'd said she couldn't trust very many people, he got the distinct impression this had to do with a man. A very specific man.

"I had this boyfriend in the circuit," she started, glancing around, but they'd left the auction and were alone under the bleachers. "He turned out to be a real jerk. Cheated on me a lot, and when I ended things with him, he turned into a stalker." She rubbed her arms as if cold, but that would be impossible this late in June, with the sun shining so brightly overhead.

Emmett couldn't imagine how anyone could cheat on someone as wonderful as Molly. He inched closer as he whispered as much, and he enjoyed that sexy blush that colored her cheeks.

"I got a restraining order against him and everything, and I couldn't trust a single thing he said to me. He said he loved me, but he hurt me. He said he wasn't cheating on me, but he was. He said he just wanted to be close to me, but really he just wanted to make sure I wasn't going out with anyone else because he was jealous and didn't trust me." She sighed and finally relaxed in his arms. "I don't—didn't trust anyone wearing a cowboy hat for a long time."

Emmett released her. "Maybe you still don't."

"I wish you would've at least pretended to listen to me back there."

"Molly, I *was* listening." He gave up the fight. "Landon wanted the Friesian. That's why I bought it." He slipped his hand into hers. "So come talk to the breeder with me, all right? We'll take that horse from zero to hero in no time—together."

She went with him, but her words marched through his mind like soldiers. She hadn't denied his suggestion that she still didn't trust anyone wearing a cowboy hat. His stomach writhed even more so than it did when he had to talk to a breeder.

## Chapter 10

Molly kept her arms clenched tight across her chest during the meeting with the breeder, though Emmett did conduct himself with power and kindness at the same time. She grudgingly admitted that the Friesian would be a great barrel racing horse, and he seemed sweet too.

As Emmett settled up, she wandered over to the horse and felt all her muscles relax. Horses held a special place in her heart, and she reached up and let him smell her before running her hand down his nose. "Hey." She looked into one of his eyes and smiled. Maybe Emmett had made a good choice with this horse, but he still hadn't listened to her.

His semi-accusation that she still didn't trust cowboys rang in her ears. Maybe she didn't. She wasn't sure.

"You ready?" Emmett joined her and let the horse sniff him too. He lifted the rope around the horse's neck and added, "I'm starving."

Molly turned, still somewhat surprised by Emmett's

good looks, the way he smelled like brown sugar and leather and fresh air, the easy smile he graced her with. "I could eat lunch." Her voice may have conducted more air than sound, and her resolve came roaring back. She straightened and coughed. "I mean, sure. It is lunchtime."

"We can leave him in the holding pen behind the stables. We'll come get 'im on the way out." Emmett clicked his tongue and tugged on the rope, bringing the Friesian with him so simply. Molly marveled at him, a wave of forgiveness washing over her.

*Can I trust him?* she wondered without consciously sending the words up as a prayer. Her step lightened and so did her heart as she followed Emmett.

"Look," she said when she caught him. "I'm sorry about earlier."

"No problem."

But it was a problem. "Maybe—I don't know. Maybe I'm still working on the trust part." She sighed. "I don't think I am, though. I trust you, Emmett."

He glanced down at her. "Am I the only man wearing a cowboy hat that you trust?"

"No," she said quickly. "I trust Landon too."

Three steps passed before Emmett started laughing, and relief produced a laugh from Molly too. He slipped his hand into hers, the earlier tension gone now. "I'm sorry too. I should've told you which horse I wanted."

"Why didn't you?"

He shrugged. "Didn't think of it."

Molly scoffed. "Let's just say I believe that." She stepped in front of him. "In the future, can you think of stuff like that? I mean, if we're gonna work together, I would think of you and you would think of me. Right?"

Emmett edged closer to her, the shade created from his cowboy hat falling over her face. "I think about you all the time, Molly." His hand landed on her hip, causing her to suck in a heated breath.

"Professionally," she said.

Emmett gave her a crooked grin. "All right."

She tipped up on her toes and kissed him quick. "All right then."

---

"It's so hot," Molly complained a couple of weeks later, wiping the sweat from her forehead as she collapsed into a chair in the shade. Tess passed her a water bottle that Molly applied directly to her face. "I don't even like parades." She glared through her sunglasses to the empty street beyond.

She'd come down to the Fourth of July parade because Megan said it was what everyone did. But it wasn't even ten o'clock yet and at least ninety degrees. On a day off, she preferred air conditioning and lounging on the couch while she watched movies, not sitting in a tiny patch of shade while various community floats went by.

Emmett handed her a package of licorice and said, "It's an hour, sweetheart. Think about the pool party."

Molly nodded, though the pool party and barbeque at the homestead also brought a measure of anxiety she couldn't swallow away. Probably because she'd have to wear a swimming suit—something she hadn't done in a long time—and hang out with all the families at Brush Creek Ranch.

She glanced at Emmett, wondering if he felt out of place among all the couples, the kids, the families. He'd been living on the ranch for eight years, so maybe not. Molly, though, was still finding her footing in the community up the canyon, and it felt like the slope was becoming more and more slippery every day she worked with Emmett, held Emmett's hand, kissed Emmett.

She was falling for him, and she couldn't even stop herself.

Every minute of the parade felt insufferable, and Molly worried more and more over her disinterest in children. She hadn't told Emmett about it. Hadn't ever really told anyone. He drove them back up the canyon and kissed her like he was falling for her too and said, "I'd invite you in, but...Tigress."

Molly smiled at him, a warm oozy smile brought on by his embrace. The past seven weeks at Brush Creek had been astronomically better than anything she could've even hoped for. She backed up and said, "I gotta change anyway."

"See you in a few minutes," he said, and Molly turned toward the cabin going up next to Emmett's. The foundation had been dug and poured and nothing more. At this rate, it would be next summer before she could move out of the basement.

She watched Emmett step onto his porch and enter his house and had the wild thought that if she married Emmett, she wouldn't need that new cabin at all.

Her throat was already dry and scratchy, but now it felt like she'd swallowed sand. A whole beach full of sand.

The sound of a truck engine broke her thoughts and she went back to the homestead as Walker and Tess pulled into the driveway next to their cabin.

The blessed air conditioning had Molly closing her eyes, sighing, and leaning against the closed front door. It smelled like baked beans and browned beef, and her stomach roared. She'd given Megan money for groceries as her donation to the potluck picnic shaping up in the backyard. She opened her eyes and found Megan carrying a tray out to the patio, and picked up several bags of chips from the counter and followed.

"Thanks, Molly." Megan gave her a genuine smile, and Molly touched her elbow to get her to stop from returning to the house for more food.

"Can I ask you a question?" Molly glanced around. The girls played on the swing set in the yard, and Landon and their son couldn't be seen.

Megan sensed something, because she paused and said, "Sure."

"Have you always—?" She swallowed, the words stuck behind a giant lump in her throat. "Wanted—wanted kids?" Her gaze flew to the twin girls swinging, one of them singing a song over and over again.

Megan blinked, the usual reaction Molly got. She backed up a step. "It's okay." She shook her head. "Never mind." She started toward the house, itching to bring out something tasty and cold. Her eyes landed on the watermelon just as Landon emerged from the hallway carrying his son.

"Molly, wait." Megan caught her just as she stepped through the door.

"No, really," Molly said, giving Megan a desperate look. The last thing she needed was Landon knowing and blabbing to Emmett. "It's okay." Molly helped get everything outside, then she escaped to the basement just as Justin and Renee showed up with their toddler.

So far from the party, Molly couldn't hear the laughter of children or the popping of soda cans, the chatter of husbands and wives or the crying of a baby. Her heart pounded like she'd been running, or like she was standing in the arena, waiting to find out if she'd won another rodeo.

She didn't go into the bedroom to change into her swim gear. She wasn't sure how much time passed before her phone went off, and when she ignored that, someone came downstairs. The footsteps indicated that it was a man, and Molly turned toward the door she'd closed, expecting Emmett to come through.

He knocked first, said, "Molly, can I come in there?"

She didn't really see what choice she had. He knew she was here, and Megan had no doubt tipped him off already. Molly got up and went to the door, twisting the knob and letting the door settle open.

Emmett stood there wearing clothes she'd never seen him in—a pair of blue floral swim trunks and a gray tank top. She'd seen him in T-shirts, his muscles bulging, but this was a whole new ballgame.

She turned away. "Hey." Back to the couch, she sank down and put her head in her hands, her breath leaking from her lungs in a long hiss.

Emmett joined her, slower and with deliberate movements. "You didn't come up to the picnic. We've already started, and you're going to miss my famous potato salad." He settled back into the couch. "Or you would've, if I hadn't saved you some." He nudged her with his elbow, and she smiled at his thoughtfulness. She'd been asking him to make her a sample of his potato salad ever since he'd bragged about it last week.

She turned toward him, her brief joy fading. "Emmett, do you want kids?"

His face blanked and his eyes flew between hers, trying to find the answer she wanted. She didn't know what to give him so he'd say something.

"I don't know," he said, his voice cautious. "Haven't really thought about it."

"Ever?"

He shook his head, his dark eyes almost wild with panic now. "I mean, I was in the rodeo, and I knew I didn't want a family then, and then I came here, and I've never—" He swallowed hard and relaxed. "Remember how you're the first woman to enter my cabin, ever?"

"Remember how I've only been inside once because of your cat?" Molly grinned though her stomach still quaked.

He chuckled. "Yeah." He sobered and took her hand in his. "So what's this really about?"

Her first instinct was to blow this off, make something up, move on. But something whispered to her to be upfront with him. "I don't want children. I never have."

## Chapter 11

Emmett didn't know how to respond to Molly. She seemed nervous yet also hopeful, and while he'd honestly never thought about having children, that didn't mean he was opposed to kids. He liked Walker and Tess's boys, and he'd been known to carry one of the twins on his shoulders when they went hiking.

"Can you not have kids?" he asked.

"I don't know. I think I can. I've just never wanted them. I'm an only child, you know? And I never liked babysitting, and I barely know what to do with kids, and—"

"All right," Emmett said, lifting his arm and tucking her into his side. "I honestly don't care." And he knew he'd spoken true as soon as the words left his mouth. "You don't want children? That's fine with me."

"Really?" She peered at him like she didn't believe.

"Sweetheart, I gave up making plans for my life when my mom walked out. I'm just livin' day to day."

She snuggled into his side, and while Megan's baked

beans and Tess's chocolate cake called to him, he stayed in the moment, with Molly, until she said she was ready to go join the party.

---

JULY PASSED with waves of heat and hours of work with the horses. Emmett had let Molly name the Friesian, and with his rich brown coat and proud features, she'd named him Double Chocolate Latte.

Emmett hated it, but in a show of working together, he'd smiled and started calling the horse Chocolate for short. Molly used all three names every time, and Emmett had learned to ignore her as the weeks passed.

The cabin next to his got walls, and a roof, and designer wood to mimic the log cabin feel. He loathed the weekends when Blake would start hammering before dawn, stop during the heat of the day, and work as late as the sun would allow, and not only because Emmett got woken up before he'd like.

As the days wore on, Emmett realized why the cabin made him cringe every time he looked at it. He didn't want Molly moving in next door. He wanted Molly to move in, period.

He'd started asking around town if someone would like to adopt a calico tabby cat. He'd kept everything quiet, so he hadn't found anyone yet. And he wasn't sure what he'd tell Molly even if he did.

Giving away the cat he loved seemed like it would take their relationship from "hey, I like you and we're great together," to "I'm thinking about marrying you." Serious.

And Emmett wasn't sure he was ready for serious. Molly spent a lot of time with the other ranch wives, leaving Emmett to seek out Grant on the evenings she was having a movie night, or a chocolate party, or a ladies' picnic in the park.

On one such evening, Emmett stomped away from the horse barn after having brushed down all three horses and cleaned up after everyone else. Molly had left two hours earlier so she could get down to the salon and get her hair done before she and Tess were meeting some friends at the bakery. What they were doing there, Emmett didn't know. The bakery closed at noon.

He left the homestead side of the lane and crossed to Cabin Row, frustrated by Blake standing outside the cabin wearing his tool belt. He'd been looking forward to an evening with ice cream, Tigress, and air conditioning. No hammering, no power tools, no noise, no conversation.

He lifted his hand in a wave, and Blake came over. "Hey, so what are you doin' tonight?"

"Nothing."

"My fiancée, Erin, is hosting this pie tasting at the bakery, and all the women will be gone. Landon's grilling, and Walker's bringing board games for the kids and cards for us. Rumor is Megan made salsa and artichoke dip before she left."

Emmett did like Megan's artichoke dip.... "I'm not really in the mood to hang out," he said.

Blake's eyebrows went up. "No? Does it bother you that Molly's gone all the time?" He exhaled and didn't wait for Emmett to answer. "Because it kind of annoys me. If Erin wants to make pie, I'd eat it." He clapped his hands together, sending dust flying into the sunny air. "She says I work too much and don't have time for pie."

Emmett paused, hearing something in Blake's voice. "Well, you do work a lot," he said. "You run the whole farm, and then you do tons of construction on the side. Isn't that how you met Erin in the first place? Fixin' up the bakery?"

Blake nodded. "If Landon didn't pay me so well, I'd tell him to get someone else to finish these cabins."

"Kind of a waste if you ask me," Emmett said.

"What do you mean?"

Emmett wasn't sure what he meant, so he just shook his head. "They meetin' at the homestead?"

"In twenty minutes."

Emmett nodded, and said, "I have to shower. I might come over."

"Better than being alone," Blake called after him, but Emmett wasn't so sure. He called Molly before he showered, but she didn't answer. He texted a couple of times after he showered, and it wasn't time for her little shindig to start yet, so he expected a response. He didn't get one. He flipped his phone over and over as he sat on the bed, glad when Tigress jumped up next to him and meowed, rubbing against his arm.

"Hey, girl." He stroked the cat while he tried to figure out if his device had gone on the fritz. It seemed to be working fine. So why hadn't she answered?

He thumbed out another message and stared at it before hitting send. He didn't want to bother her, and his heart seized when he realized how many times he'd contacted her without a response.

Her silence was her answer, and it was loud and clear. He suddenly didn't want to be alone with his cat and Molly's cold shoulder, so he got himself over to Landon's, where the lights were cheery and the food delicious. He loaded up with cookies and milk and went to find the other single man on the ranch—Grant Ford.

The man had black sideburns that went almost all the way to his chin, and they made Emmett smile every time. "Hey."

Grant gave him an easy smile, the way he always did. "Horses behaving?"

"As much as the cows probably are."

"Which means they're not."

Emmett dunked his cookie into his milk and chuckled, everything in him starting to loosen. He'd taken one bite when Grant said, "So I started dating a teacher down in town," with a fair bit of swagger.

The glass of milk Emmett held slipped in his fingers. "You did?" he asked around a mouthful of cookie and milk.

Grant nodded, seemingly pleased with himself. "It's new. Maybe a couple of weeks."

"Great," Emmett said. "Great." But it didn't feel great to Emmett. It felt like Grant was going to fall in love with this teacher and leave Emmett the only one at the ranch without anyone to come home to.

He set his cookies aside and checked his phone. Nothing from Molly.

———

Emmett saddled Chocolate the following morning and tethered Beauty to the Friesian before taking them down the dirt road and out through the fields. Molly hadn't called, not even when she'd gotten in last night. Not even when he'd texted to ask her if they should train Chocolate that morning or go riding.

The radio silence suffocated him, and he'd made his own decision. He didn't like being left out of the conversation, and he'd realized how hurt she'd been when they'd gone to Cheyenne.

He glanced back the way he'd come, but the homestead and Cabin Row were distant dots on the horizon. The stream was merely a trickle now, but the horses still managed to find something to drink. Emmett sat on the bank, with the sun on his back and his thoughts as far and wide as the horizon.

He wasn't even sure what was going on with Molly, because she hadn't called or texted. He sighed; he really wanted to stop thinking about her. Three months ago, he'd come out here and been happy and peaceful. He hadn't wanted for anything then. Hadn't even considered that something was missing in his life.

Now, he felt a hole in his soul that wouldn't go away, and he had no idea how to fix it. He stayed out in the wild quiet until the heat of the day started to oppress him. Then he collected the horses from the fields where they'd wandered and took them back to the ranch.

He knew something was up when he came down the road and found Tess and Megan standing in front of his cabin, both of them pacing. Blake wasn't working on the cabins anymore, and everything on the ranch seemed muted.

"Tess?" he called, and she spun toward him, worry mixing with relief when she saw and recognized him. "What is it?"

She strode toward him, Megan following her. They reached him at the same time. "It's Molly," she said. "Well, her dad. He collapsed last night, and she left the bakery almost right after we got there."

Confusion drew his eyebrows into a V. "Why didn't she call me?"

"She did." Tess looked at Megan. "Twice. You didn't answer."

Emmett shook his head and pulled out his phone. "No, look. I haven't heard from her."

Tess looked at the phone for a fraction of a second. "Okay, but she called."

Desperation pulled through Emmett. He wanted them to understand he hadn't blown off the calls, but it wasn't worth arguing over. "When you say she left, what does that mean?"

"It means she's gone," Megan said.

"For good?" Emmett asked, the reins he held in his hand suddenly weighing a hundred pounds.

"That's what she said." Tess drew him into a hug. "Oh, honey, I'm so sorry."

## Chapter 12

Molly slept in a hotel in a suburb of Denver, after an exhausting eight-hour drive. After five hours, she hit the road again near nine o'clock, frustrated that all of her messages and calls to Emmett had gone unanswered. He'd called her, and she'd sent it to voicemail because Erin had just brought out the key lime tarts, and the ladies were in a chorus of squeals over the treats.

Her world had gone from carefree and full of laughter to terrifying with a single phone call, and she'd left town without anything but her truck, her purse, and the clothes she'd been wearing.

She flexed her fingers on the steering wheel and watched the clock until it clicked to ten, the appointed time when she told her mother she'd call. Out of sheer desperation, she tried Emmett again.

His phone only rang once before going to voicemail, and she wondered if the cell tower out on the ranch had gone down. She couldn't quite explain any other reason why he wouldn't answer, other than he was angry at her for not answering.

"That makes no sense," she said. They'd traded calls and texts before. All summer long, in fact. But she couldn't help worrying over him—and it wasn't because he wasn't answering.

It was because she wasn't returning to Brush Creek. She couldn't worry about her belongings there; she suspected she could ask Megan to box up her clothes and shoes and mail them to her. It was fourteen hours from Omaha to Brush Creek, and it seemed silly to take a twenty-eight hour round-trip just to get a few blouses and jeans.

Still, she felt a keen sense of loss over her clothes. Over the three horses she'd grown to love. Over Emmett.

She sighed, startled out of her feelings by the ringing of her phone. She fumbled it in her haste to answer, disappointed her mother started talking instead of Emmett.

"Your father is stable," she said, a sigh accompanying the words. Mom sounded so tired and Molly wanted to be close by to support her. She thought about her mom planning a funeral by herself, and a sob crept up her throat.

"How are you?" Molly choked out.

"Surviving."

"What are his chance of recovering this time?"

"The same as always." Mom's voice lowered when she continued with "But honestly, Molly, I don't think he'll leave the hospital again." How she could say the words with such steadiness, Molly didn't know.

"I'm on my way," she said. "I'm only five hours out. Tell him, okay? Will you tell him I'm coming?" Molly wiped her eyes, glad she didn't have to be strong in this moment, relieved no one was with her to see her cry.

She hung up with her mom and took an extra second to blink. "Please don't let him die before I get there." She kept a steady, silent prayer going as the miles continued to roll by.

An hour out, she grabbed something for lunch so she could get right to her father when she arrived at the hospital. She'd barely set her truck on the highway again when her phone rang.

When she saw Emmett's name on the screen, she swung onto the shoulder, unable to focus on driving and speak with him at the same time.

"Emmett," she said.

"Hey, sweetheart," he said. His voice sounded off, but she couldn't quite place the emotions it carried. "Where are you?"

"About an hour outside of Omaha."

She could imagine him nodding his head, short little bursts of movement. He'd be swallowing about now, and probably glancing away as he tried to figure out what to say.

"I'm sorry I didn't answer," he said. "Something happened with my phone. I didn't get any messages or calls, and when Tess found me and told me what was going on, I restarted my phone and reset it, and they all came through." He exhaled, the sound heavy and full of frustration. "I've never had thirteen unread texts before." He chuckled, but it sounded off.

"Emmett—" She didn't know what else to say.

"I wish I'd have gotten your call. I would've come with you."

"I know."

"Is it true you're not coming back?"

"I don't know right now, Emmett."

"You don't know?"

"I don't know what my dad will be like, and I can't imagine leaving my mom here alone if he—if he—"

"But I thought you didn't want to stay in Omaha. You told me that you just couldn't stay there."

She had said that. She had felt suffocated in her hometown, in that same house where she'd grown up, with her ill father and her broken mother. The thought of staying in Nebraska made her stomach roll, and the thought of never seeing Emmett again, never smelling his skin, never kissing him, caused every muscle in her body to tighten.

"Can I call you later?" she asked. "After I see my dad and talk to my mom?"

"Sure, of course." He cleared his throat. "Should I come to Omaha?"

Her first instinct was to say no. She didn't want him to see her in such distress. At the same time, she could use someone strong to rely on. She ended up saying, "I don't know."

"Think about it," he said.

Her brain whirred, settling on several things at once. "You can't leave the horses. We just started with Double Chocolate Latte, and you're meeting with that cowgirl from Austin on Tuesday."

"I'm sure Landon could handle the meeting. He has to approve all the sales anyway."

"You'll be heartbroken without Beauty."

He scoffed and said, "Heartbroken? She's just a horse."

"She's your favorite horse." She managed to smile and she eased back onto the road, able to drive and talk now.

"You're my favorite," he said, and her heart stuttered.

"I have to go." Her voice came out way too high and she ended the call before he could say anything else.

When she got to the hospital, her mom met her in the lobby. "Mom." Molly took a big breath and kept the tears dormant. Her mom trembled in her arms, and Molly held her, soothed her, was the strong one in the relationship just like she'd always been.

"How is he?" She held her at arm's length and looked down at her mom.

"They just took him in for some tests. He should be back soon, and he'll be awake."

"Let's go up then." Molly pasted on a smile and let her mom lead her up to the fourth floor. Molly couldn't seem to sit still, and there was only one chair anyway. She perched in the wide windowsill, her foot bouncing, bouncing, bouncing.

Mom chattered about the roses Dad had planted and how he spent hours everyday pruning them and dallying around outside. "How he deals with the heat and humidity is beyond me." Mom fanned herself and watched the TV mounted above the door. "But he does love those roses."

"How are the pink lemonade ones doing? The ones I gave him for Father's Day a few years ago?" Molly had really wanted to give him something he'd be able to look at and see her.

"He brings a new bloom in everyday. They really smell like lemonade."

A ghost of a smile drifted across Molly's face. "I remember."

Several minutes later, the door opened and two nurses wheeled in her father. Molly shot to her feet, that lump in her throat clogging all the words and making speaking impossible.

"Look, Gene. Molly's here."

Dad's eyes wandered, finally landing on hers. He smiled and lifted one veined hand toward her. She couldn't believe how old he looked, how frail lying in the bed, how much he'd aged in the single summer she'd been gone.

Should she have stayed? Been with him in his last days?

*These aren't his last days*, she told herself firmly, straightening her shoulders and taking his hand in between both of hers. *And you're here now.*

"Hey, Daddy." She leaned in and took a breath of him, getting the hint of his unique smell of blooms and butterscotch beneath the antiseptic scent of the hospital. "How are you feeling?"

"Oh, just fine." His voice sounded like he'd gargled with glass, and there was hardly anything about him that she remembered. This wasn't the man she knew growing up. That man kicked a soccer ball with her when she was eight years old. He'd taken her to her first horseback riding lesson —and every one after it. He'd come to all her rodeo events her first year, and would've the second too if not for the cancer diagnosis.

"These nurses, they overreact."

Molly glanced at one of them, who gave her a knowing smile. "I'm sure they do."

"You didn't have to come all this way."

"Dad, you're—" She cut off. "I wanted to come see you guys. It's been a few months."

"How are things going on the ranch?" Mom asked.

"Just fine," she said, not wanting to talk about the ranch, or horses, or anything remotely related to ranches or horses right now. She certainly couldn't voice that she'd found what she wanted to do with the rest of her life in training barrel racing horses. Not right now. And she didn't want to talk about her newfound faith, because it felt so far from her right now. Almost like God had forgotten about her, or given her something wonderful only to snatch it away in the next moment.

She wouldn't mention Emmett, because if she did, she'd break down, and that was not an option, not with her father resting in a hospital bed and her mom barely conscious in the chair beside him. No, Molly needed to be the strong one here, and if that meant keeping her life in Brush Creek close to the vest, she'd do it.

---

A WEEK LATER, Molly entered the kitchen where she used to eat Lucky Charms and found her mom standing at the window, a mug of steaming coffee in her hand.

"Morning," she said, pulling a mug down from the cupboard and filling it with liquid caffeine. She hadn't been sleeping well, and drinking coffee was the only way she'd make it through the day. It was probably also why she laid awake at night.

That, and her worry about her father, and her increasing misery over Emmett. He'd texted a couple of times, but he'd stuck to business. He'd sold Beauty to the cowgirl on Tuesday, and he had two meetings with potential buyers for Hurricane lined up at the end of the month. He didn't mention Double Chocolate Latte, and Molly found herself wondering after the Friesian. She'd grown attached to the horse in the month she'd worked with him.

She didn't ask. She filled her messages with exclamation points and smiling emoticons so he wouldn't know how unhappy she was. She spooned sugar into her coffee and joined her mom at the window.

Mom finally turned from the world outside and said, "Oh, good morning, dear," as if Molly hadn't already said good morning and hadn't spent the last couple of minutes banging around the kitchen.

Worry needled through her, but she supposed Mom hadn't been sleeping either. Spending hours that felt like days in the hospital didn't help, and nothing felt real in Molly's life anymore.

"Who's Emmett?" Mom asked, jumpstarting Molly's heart.

"What?"

She glanced at Molly's phone on the counter. "He's texted a couple of times this morning."

"Oh." Molly waved her hand. "He's my boss. Well, not really my boss." A nervous giggle left her lips. "He and I train the horses together on the ranch." She took a giant sip of her coffee and burnt her tongue and the roof of her mouth and all the way down her throat. She coughed, which finally alerted Mom to something suspicious.

"You work with him?"

"I work with a lot of cowboys. Well, not a lot." She

cringed at the way she kept saying things and then correcting herself. "A few. My boss is a cowboy."

"You seeing anyone? Maybe one of those cowboys? Maybe Emmett?"

Molly scoffed and pushed out one laugh. "Why do you think that?"

Mom glanced at the phone, and Molly turned to pick it up. Emmett had finally broken from business to say *I miss you. Have you thought any more about me coming to Omaha?*

She had thought more about it, and the more brain space she dedicated to it, the worse the idea sounded. What would he possibly do here? She didn't need to work because of her winnings in the rodeo, but she was bored out of her mind. She'd taken to her father's gardens just to fill the hours with something that felt semi-meaningful.

She lowered the phone and looked at her mom. "Yes, I'm dating Emmett."

A smile as wide as the sky graced her mom's face. "That's wonderful." As quickly as the grin had appeared, it faded. "Is that why you've been so miserable here?"

Molly shrugged. She hadn't cried in front of her parents. She'd keep the tears for her pillow and only after she was sure Mom was asleep.

"Are you going to let him come?"

"I don't know, Mom."

"Do you love him?"

Molly flinched at the question. She wasn't even sure she knew how to love a man. She thought she'd been in love with Clay, and that had gone terribly wrong. Or he was terribly wrong. Or maybe she was. She still wasn't sure what she'd seen in him now, especially when she considered Emmett and his calm personality, his quick laughter, his kind soul.

With a jolt, she realized that she did love him. She turned toward her mom as the sunlight poured through the window, almost like a beacon from heaven. "I think so."

Her mom's tired, crinkly face smoothed and lit up. Molly was able to see the woman she'd grown up with, who she loved, who she'd come here for, in that single moment. "Are you going to let him come, then?"

Molly looked at the phone clenched in her hand. The sun went behind a cloud, and everything in Molly's mind scattered. "I don't know. He's really busy on the ranch right now. It's almost the harvest, which all the cowboys help with, and he's finishing up with one horse and just starting another one."

Mom nodded like what Molly had said wasn't just an excuse. She sipped her coffee and looked out into the yard, with its dozens of rose bushes and lanes of emerald green grass. Thunder sounded overhead, making the light even dimmer.

"Maybe you should let him decide." Mom put her hand on Molly's forearm and squeezed. "I'm going to go shower and then we'll go over to the hospital. Your father loves the rain and he'll want me to wheel him to the balcony."

Molly nodded, her words stuck somewhere deep inside her chest. She loved her parents, and she wanted—*needed*—to be here with them right now.

But did that mean Emmett couldn't be with her too?

She pressed her eyes closed and searched her soul, the way she'd learned to do this summer as Pastor Peters stood at the pulpit and said wonderful things that rang true in her heart. She loved Emmett Graves, and she didn't want to let her father's illness keep them apart. She had to be here for right now, but maybe not forever.

And if she didn't cling to Emmett now, she could lose him forever.

Her eyes popped open and her fingers flew across the screen.

## Chapter 13

Emmett picked up the phone when it rang, though he usually didn't do such things while working with his horses. He felt utterly abandoned since Molly had left last week and he'd sold Beauty. He'd spent all day Sunday and Monday with her, telling her she was going to love her new owners, and that he'd be there at her first professional rodeo.

The horse didn't answer back—likely didn't even know what he was saying—but he liked to think she would comfort him, tell him it was okay, that she was ready to start winning championships and that she'd thank him in her acceptance speeches.

"Hey," he said to the pastor's wife, Alison. "Any news?"

"My daughter in Elkhorn will take your cat. She's thrilled because she'd been trying to find a birthday present for her daughter, who loves cats."

Emmett's chest expanded and collapsed as he breathed. He couldn't believe he was getting rid of Tigress, the one creature who hadn't left him yet. On his next breath, he reminded himself that if he wanted Molly in his life, he couldn't have Tigress. And this was weeks in the making.

"Great," he finally said. "I can drive over to Elkhorn in the morning."

"Don't be ridiculous. It's an hour away," she said. "Heather is coming here next weekend. I'll take Tigress until then. I know you boys are busy with the harvest at this time of year."

As if Emmett's heart wasn't already in his boots. He hated the harvest, as did most cowboys. Blake especially. But Emmett pulled his weight around the ranch, and if they wanted to feed their cattle and horses all winter, they needed the hay.

"All right," Emmett said. "I'll bring her down to you tonight. Does that work?"

"It works."

Emmett hung up with Alison, more depressed than ever. At the same time, he thanked the Lord for helping his plans to go so smoothly. He'd texted Molly that morning about coming to Omaha, and she hadn't answered yet. But when she did, Emmett wanted to be ready.

He already had a bag packed and all he needed was a text. Or a phone call. Heck, he'd take an email or a Facebook message at this point. Something.

He couldn't imagine the stress Molly was feeling, so he tried not to be impatient or frustrated with her lack of communication. He hadn't exactly been Mr. Communicative himself, sticking to facts about the horses and the ranch until this morning.

Leaving his phone on the fence post, he moved back into the training circle to where Chocolate waited. The horse kept his head down as Emmett approached, exactly how he'd been trained to do.

"C'mon, boy," Emmett whispered and held out his hand. The horse should come to him, treat or no treat, and he did. Chocolate had been down since Molly's departure too, and now Emmett gave him an affectionate pat on the neck. "I miss her, too."

He sighed and swung into the saddle. He guided Chocolate with his reins and legs to move within four feet of the barrel he'd put out. He forced the horse to keep his head down, and when Chocolate performed his duty, Emmett took a baby carrot from the bag attached to the saddle horn and rewarded the horse.

Over and over, at varying speeds, did Emmett make Chocolate approach the barrel, circle it, and come out straight. He'd have to do that three times in under fifteen seconds to win a barrel race, and Emmett was nothing if not meticulous with his horse training.

The work was mindless, and Emmett loved it. Loved the smell of the country and dust and horsehair. Loved the feel of the animal beneath him and the sound of hooves on packed earth.

His phone sounded, and he swung Chocolate toward the fence post. The screen was black by the time they got there, but a blue light flashed. Emmett picked up his phone and saw a text from Courtney Davis.

His throat tightened and then released. Courtney was interested in buying Hurricane, and her family had a lot of money to make sure she was equipped with the best horse possible. He confirmed her appointment for the following Wednesday, and he put a reminder in his calendar to spend

Tuesday afternoon bathing Hurricane and getting him pretty for the barrel racer.

Not the text he wanted, but progress, he supposed. He shoved the phone in the bag with the carrots and got back to work.

After lunch, Grant went with Emmett from the homestead to pasture while Emmett detailed what he'd done with Chocolate's training that morning. Emmett had asked Landon if he could get someone to take over the Friesian's training as he'd been hoping and praying with every cell in his body that Molly would ask him to come to Nebraska.

They approached Chocolate in the pasture, where Emmett had left him before heading to lunch, when Emmett realized he'd left his phone in the bag on the saddle —which now hung in the tack room.

"You coax him over here," Emmett said. "He should come to you whenever you say. I'll go grab the equipment." He practically ran back to the horse barn, his hopes soaring toward the clouds like someone had inflated them with helium.

He wasn't sure he could stand another minute of living here at Brush Creek without Molly. Or at least the prospect of seeing Molly soon.

His phone flashed blue and green when he finally got to it, and he'd missed a call and a string of texts from Molly.

*I do want you to come to Omaha.*

*But I understand if you can't.*

*I know the harvest is soon, and I know you're working on a deal for Hurricane.*

*But when you can.*

*I don't know how long I'll be here, but my dad isn't doing well. If he dies....*

*Call me when you get a sec.*

His heart beat behind his eyes, in his ears, in the back of his throat. She wanted him to come to Omaha.

She wanted him.

He hit the call button without seeing if she'd left a message and waited while it rang.

"Hey," she said, her voice hushed.

"Can you talk?" he asked.

"Give me a minute." Scuffling came through the line, then a bang, and then her heavy sigh. "All right."

"I got your texts. I'm already packed."

She didn't answer, and Emmett checked to make sure his phone was still working. Since its malfunction last week, he didn't trust the thing.

"Thank you," she said just as he put the device back to his ear. "I need you."

"I don't know when I can come," he said. "I need to talk to Landon, and I already set up an appointment with a rider for Hurricane on Wednesday."

"Whenever is fine," she said. "My dad's—he's not— well, he's not doing well. The doctor told us this morning that he doesn't think he'll last another week." Her voice broke on the last word, and Emmett's heart cracked. He needed to be with her. Now.

"I'll be there," he said. "As fast as I can, I'll be there."

She sniffled. "It's fine, really. *I'm* fine. I—"

"You are not," he said firmly, glancing toward the ceiling. "It's okay to not be okay."

Her silence meant she was too choked up to answer,

and he imagined her nodding while she wiped her beautiful eyes.

"I have a few things to take care of." He grabbed the saddle and other equipment he needed to saddle Chocolate and started down the aisle of the horse barn. "I'll call you tonight and let you know when I can come, all right?"

"All right," she said. "Thank you."

He paused in the doorway, one foot in sunlight and the other still in shade. He swallowed hard and said, "Molly?"

"Yeah?"

"I love you." He cleared his throat. "You hang on, all right?"

"Uh huh," she said.

Before he could make a bigger fool of himself, he said, "All right. Talk to you later," and hung up. He let his arm drop to his side, gripping the phone until his bones hurt. The device vibrated and he looked at it.

*I love you too.*

A grin broke onto his face and everything inside him finally felt free. He whooped, laughed, and hurried back to the pasture so he could get Grant working with Chocolate.

———

Two weeks later, Emmett finally loaded his packed bag into his truck and turned to embrace Tess. She wept as she hugged him, and Walker handed him a cooler full of her concoctions.

"You're staying in Denver tonight, right?" she asked for at least the twentieth time since he'd shown up at her and Walker's place and asked for their help. Landon had wanted him to give Grant a couple more weeks of training with Chocolate, and the owner really did need all his cowboys' help to get the harvest in.

Everything was finally in place, including Emmett's hotel reservation in Denver that night. "You made the reservation," Emmett said with a grin. "So yes, I'm staying in Denver tonight."

"And Molly's dad hasn't passed away yet, right?"

Emmett set his jaw and shook his head. "He's holding on, despite what the doctors keep saying. He's still in the hospital, and Molly is exhausted."

Tess nodded. "I talked to her yesterday."

"Then why are you standin' here askin' the poor man questions?" Walker rolled his eyes and clapped Emmett on the shoulder. "Drive carefully, Emmett." He put his arm around Tess's shoulders and eased her away from the truck so Emmett could get in.

He left Brush Creek, hoping he'd be back really soon—with Molly. But he just didn't know, as he'd told Landon. Landon had assured him there would always be a job here for him—and Molly too—and to keep him updated.

Emmett ate burgers and fries and slept poorly in the hotel. By the time he arrived in Omaha, he thought his nerves would explode from his body and demand to be transplanted into someone with much less anxiety.

He'd called Molly an hour ago, and she'd said she'd be waiting in the lobby. His cowboy boots made clunking noises on the tile as he walked and walked from the parking garage. He finally saw a large rotunda up ahead—and a gorgeous redhead with curly hair.

"Molly," came out of his mouth before he could tell it

not to. He was much too far away for her to hear him, and yet she lifted her head and searched the hallway where he was almost running now.

She leapt to her feet when she finally saw him, and he did break into a jog then.

"Emmett!" She met him at the edge of the rotunda and he swept her off her feet with a booming laugh that filled the space. The feel of her in his arms was absolutely right, and Emmett finally felt like the hole that had been in his life had been plugged.

He set her on her feet and took her face in his hands, feeling her cheekbones and along her jaw. "You're beautiful," he said, gazing at her with all the love he felt. "I missed you so much."

She grinned at him, and though he saw the exhaustion in the lines around her eyes, she seemed happy to see him. "You sold Hurricane all right?"

"No horse talk," he said, leaning down to kiss her. This union of their mouths was sweeter than the first, as Emmett had thought he'd lost her. He rejoiced to be holding her again, tasting the coffee she'd recently drank, and smelling that pineappley scent that belonged uniquely to her.

"I love you," he whispered against her lips before claiming them again.

She clung to him like she needed his frame to keep her upright, and Emmett was overjoyed to provide for her whatever she wanted. She kissed him back with all the passion she'd always had and murmured, "I love you too," before tucking her head against his chest.

"My mom's dying to meet you," she said, stepping back

and threading her arm through his elbow. "Are you ready for that?"

"I was born ready for that." He grinned at her and she smiled back, and Emmett wondered how he'd been happy before meeting Molly. How he'd gone home to his cabin without her. How he'd felt settled when she wasn't his.

He knew now that he could only be happy with her, and that wherever she was would be home to him.

# Chapter 14

Molly poked her head into the hospital room, hoping her dad was awake and would be able to remember meeting Emmett. She feared it would be the one and only time he did, but she stuffed that worry to the bottom of her feet.

She found both of her parents standing at the window, which shot surprise right through her. "Mom?"

Mom turned from the window and took in Emmett and Molly before a smile bloomed on her face, showing that younger version of her that Molly loved. "Molly, this must be your Emmett." She turned back to Molly's dad. "Gene, he's here."

Emmett's fingers on hers tightened and then released as he stepped into the room and crossed to them. "Hello, sir. Ma'am."

Mom twittered like a bird. "Oh, don't be so formal. I'm Hattie and this is Gene."

Emmett shifted his feet, moving forward and then backward, and then drawing both of her parents into a hug. "It's so good to meet you," he said.

Molly watched her mom close her eyes and hold onto one of Emmett's wide shoulders, smiling for all she was worth. "So good to meet you too."

He stepped back and clapped his hands. "So. Childhood stories. I've heard precious little." He shot her a glance over his shoulder and grinned wolfishly. He helped her father back into bed and proceeded to wait on everyone hand and foot for the rest of the day.

Molly let him, because it was so nice to have someone else there who could shoulder the load. Someone else to do things, give advice, stay stoic. Once, she caught his eye as he sat in the window and listened to her mother outline how she'd gone out of the fifth grade spelling bee on the word *reservoir*, and he gave her an adoring smile that melted her heart.

---

LATER THAT NIGHT, once they were finally alone, Molly asked him about the ranch, the horses, his cat.

"I gave Tigress to another family," he said like it was nothing.

Molly tensed. "Just for a little while, right?"

"No, there was a ten-year-old girl who wanted a cat, and her mom gave her Tigress for her birthday." He leaned over and unzipped his bag, pulling out a pair of gym shorts. "Bathroom's down the hall, right?"

Molly jumped in front of the door, though it was open. Just the thought of him sleeping here at her parents' house had her nerves in a knot. She thought she hadn't been able to sleep before, but she feared tonight would be her worst night yet.

She shook her head, her jaw set. "I can't believe you gave away your cat."

"You're allergic," Emmett said, stepping closer, his fingers tripping over hers.

"You could've just had someone watch her while you came here."

He lifted his eyes to hers. "And then what? When we go back to Brush Creek, what would you have done? Lived next door?" He scoffed and returned his attention to his luggage.

"I have no idea when I'll go back to Brush Creek."

"But you will," he said.

"Maybe."

He turned toward her deliberately. "There's no 'maybe' about it, Molly. I'm staying here with you for as long as you need me. As long as you're here. Then we'll go back to Brush Creek and start training barrel horses again. Landon said we could."

"It could be months and months."

"So what?" He inched a little closer, his eyes dark, edged, and dangerous.

"So you're going to live in my parents' guest bedroom until then?" She lifted her chin and folded her arms.

"No, probably not," he admitted. "It won't be kosher after we're engaged."

Before Molly could blink, breathe, or vocalize, he displayed a black box with the lid cracked. A diamond sat nestled in the cream-colored silk insert.

Emmett dropped to one knee. "Molly Brady, will you marry me?"

Fireworks popped in her bloodstream. She half-laughed, half-cried. Gazing down on him, her heart swelled and swelled and swelled.

"Yes," she finally said, a giggle escalating through her throat into a high-pitched squeal.

He straightened and she threw herself into his arms. He laughed as he caught her around the waist and kissed her. He slid the ring on her finger and looked at her with such hope and joy shining in his eyes, she couldn't help but kiss him again.

---

Daddy held on for three more days before he passed away with all three of them in the room, one hand clutched in Molly's and one in Mom's. Emmett wept with them though he'd just met her father, and the next several days blurred as Molly helped her mom take care of all the funeral arrangements.

Emmett brought them food and insisted they go to bed on time. He had coffee ready in the morning, and he mowed the lawn and cleaned out the garage during the day. He visited with the neighbors and accepted the food from the ladies at the church. He took care of everyone and everything, and Molly loved him even more for it.

She mourned in stages, and when she finally admitted that her father would not be walking her down the aisle as she married Emmett, she broke down and cried. She'd mostly quieted by the time Emmett found her in the backyard, a pink lemonade rose clutched in her fingers.

"Come on now, sweetheart." He tucked her into his side and rubbed her upper arm. "I brought pizza. Plain pepperoni. Your favorite."

She stayed curled into him for another thirty minutes before she dared go in the house, where her mother met her with, "I think I should sell the house."

Molly froze though the smell of tomato sauce and cheese and spicy pepperoni tickled her nose. "Sell the house?"

Her mom glanced around at the cupboards that hadn't changed in two decades, the paint that Molly had helped with her junior year in college, and the carpet that had definitely seen better days. "Yeah. I don't think I can live here without your father. It's too big. And the yard. All those rose bushes." She turned her eyes on Molly, who didn't know what to say.

Obvious discomfort showed in her mom's eyes, and Molly didn't want to leave her here alone. She couldn't even imagine living here without her dad, between these walls that held so many memories.

Molly drew a deep breath and met Emmett's eyes and then her mom's. "Can we pack up the pink lemonade rose bush and take it to Brush Creek?"

---

Two weeks later Molly drove her truck with her mother in the passenger seat, while Emmett drove his hitched to a fifteen-foot moving trailer. She had never been so tired. Cleaning out a two-thousand-square-foot house and consulting with her mother on every item had really sapped her.

Not to mention the painting, the staging, the multiple showings before the house went under contract. They'd signed the paperwork just last night, and Molly had never felt such relief.

Emmett had Tess and Megan looking for a simple apartment or a small cottage in town for Mom, and she'd called Megan and asked her if she could have her room back in the basement until she and Emmett were married.

He wanted a ranch wedding, but Molly wasn't sure about having the ceremony outside of the church. She said she'd think about it, and the hours passed to Denver while her mind circled little else.

By the time she pulled in beside Emmett at a steakhouse in Denver, she'd decided. "Hey," she said when he got out of the cab. "Let's do it."

"Do what?"

"Get married on the ranch."

His face blanched and then split into a grin. "Yeah?"

"Yeah. What are the chances we can get Beauty to make an appearance?"

His joy visibly faded, and she laughed. "I was kidding." She stepped into his arms and tilted her head up at him.

He received her, wrapping his arms around her waist without focusing on her. "I do miss Beauty."

"Who's Beauty?" Molly's mom asked. "Not some other woman, right?"

Both Molly and Emmett broke into laughter, and with a decision made, Molly started mentally planning her wedding with the best horseman she knew.

## Chapter 15

Emmett drew comfort from Double Chocolate Latte while he waited for the wedding to start. It had been a very long month back on the ranch, but Molly didn't want Halloween anywhere near her wedding date.

He wasn't sure how November fifth wasn't anywhere near Halloween, but according to Molly—and every other woman at the ranch—it was three hundred and sixty days away instead of just five.

Emmett didn't care. He was just ready to get married. Ready to wake up with Molly at his side and ready to make her dinner after they spent the day riding horses. Walker entered the barn and locked the door behind him. When Emmett cocked his eyebrow, Walker said, "Tess is sure I can't straighten your tie and make sure you're ready to get married."

Emmett grinned. "She could've come in."

"Trust me, you don't want to open that can of worms."

Walker grinned and leaned against an empty stall. "She lectured me for ten minutes about my best man duties." He scanned Emmett and adjusted the tie. "So, are you ready to get married?"

"One hundred percent." He glanced over Walker's shoulder. "How close are we?"

"Ten minutes, give or take." Walker moved over to Chocolate and stroked his hand down the horse's mane. "Most people are here. Your dad's right in the front row."

Emmett's heart kicked out an extra beat. His father and two brothers had arrived earlier in the week, and they gawked at everything on the ranch like they'd never seen a horse or a barn before. They were leaving today, after the wedding, at the same time Emmett and Molly were headed to California for a honeymoon on the beach.

His father had said he'd told Emmett's mother about the wedding, but she hadn't come. Emmett hadn't even known his parents still spoke to each other. Part of him wanted to know where his mother had been all these years, and the other part liked the bliss ignorance brought. He hadn't asked. Molly's mom lived just down the canyon, and she seemed to like having Emmett around. He figured he'd survived this long without his mother; now that he had Molly, he didn't need much of anything else.

He took a deep breath, the scent of horses and hay and his own cologne calming him further. He'd suggested getting married on horseback, but Molly had nixed the idea. She said she wanted to be right next to him, not maneuvering her horse, when they got married.

Someone knocked on the door, and Walker turned toward Emmett. "It's time."

Emmett straightened his shoulders and tugged on the end of his jacket sleeves. The weather had been cooperating so far, and he stepped into crisp fall air and a bright sun. He adjusted his hat as the size of the crowd came into view. The entire front yard was filled with chairs, and streamers blew in the wind. He moved through the people, shaking hands and exchanging hugs until he made it to the arch at the end of an aisle that started at the front door of the homestead.

Pastor Peters further calmed Emmett. Molly had loved the pastor from the first moment she'd heard him talk, and Emmett's fondness for the man had grown because of that. He stood behind an altar that Landon had carved from a fallen tree on the ranch and an antique bicycle off to the right completed the rustic look.

In the front row, Molly's mother manned the CD player that played pretty piano music. She stopped it and started the wedding march, and Emmett turned toward the homestead at the same time everyone else did. Molly appeared, her dress full and billowy from the waist down. The bodice was fitted and left her shoulders bare, causing Emmett to swallow hard and thank the Lord for his good fortune in meeting someone like Molly. He was grateful he'd somehow convinced her to marry him, and as she stepped toward him, a shock of emotion tumbled through his system.

His throat tightened and he could barely breathe. He hoped he could make it through the ceremony and say what he needed to say. Molly reached him, and Landon passed her to Emmett, who leaned close and inhaled her pineapple and coconut scent.

"Mm," he said. "You ready?"

"Yes. You?" She looked at him with apprehension, like he might change his mind and bolt.

"Let's do this." He faced Pastor Peters, who began the ceremony in that joyful, soothing voice of his.

When it was Emmett's turn to speak, he delivered his vows with passion and emotion, just the way he'd hoped to. Molly teared up when she spoke, which made tears prick Emmett's eyes.

"I never told you that I came to Brush Creek to avoid cowboys," she started. "I blew you off the first time we met, and I'm grateful every day that God saw fit to give me a second chance to take a first look at you." Her chin wobbled, but she continued with, "I love you, Emmett Graves, and I'm thrilled to be the wife of a cowboy."

He leaned closer, a grin tugging at the corners of his mouth. "I'm really a horseman," he said in a fake whisper. The audience laughed, and Molly giggled.

She moved to kiss him, but Pastor Peters said, "Wait. Not quite yet," which also prompted a laugh from everyone behind them.

A few more words were said, and then the pastor said, "I now pronounce you husband and wife." He beamed at Molly. "Now you can kiss him."

She threw herself into his arms and Emmett was more than happy to seal their marriage with a kiss. For something he never thought he'd wanted, he sure was happy to have Molly here with him on the ranch.

As he turned and lifted Molly's hand to a roaring applause, Emmett finally felt like he was home.

---

Read on for a sneak peek at **SCHOOLED BY THE COWBOY**, the next book in the bestselling Brush Creek Cowboys series.

# Sneak Peek! Schooled by the Cowboy Chapter One

Principal Shannon Sharpe was aware of exactly how long the cowboy had been standing at the corner of the building. It was her job to know, and though he'd never done anything, he couldn't keep coming around school grounds and watching.

She'd employed her excellent detective skills to figure out who he was. After all, she didn't want to alienate a parent, but she also couldn't risk the safety of her students and teachers if the man had a restraining order against him or wasn't allowed to see his child.

Thankfully, this cowboy didn't fit any of that. Wasn't married. Had never been married. Had no children.

He'd dated one of her second grade teachers for a brief time last year, and Shannon suspected the poor guy wasn't over beautiful, bubbly, blonde Claire.

*Still*, she told herself as the children continued to practice their dance festival pieces. *He can't just show up at school and stare. If a parent saw....*

She turned away from the sixth grade class doing the

cha-cha and clicked her way toward the far corner of the building. Her necklaces jangled as her heels made sharp noises against the blacktop. She fiddled with the hummingbird ring on her middle finger as she approached, the only sign of her nerves.

"Sir?" She paused out of his reach and touched her dangly, sparkling earrings.

The man startled as if he hadn't noticed her approach. He had black hair that extended into a pair of sexy sideburns all the way to his chin. His eyes reminded her of her favorite black tea, and his quick smile made her relax her weight onto her right foot.

"Ma'am." He swept his cowboy hat off and tipped his head in acknowledgement. Shannon wished she was meeting him at one of the town's summer activities, or the community country line dances, or a church function, because he was gorgeous. Tall and broad, with biceps that showed his muscles when he folded them across his chest.

"Can I ask what you're doing here?" she asked, her voice betraying her frantically beating heart. She told herself she would never react like this to a parent, but she already knew this man didn't fit that bill. So her erratic pulse and sudden hopes were justified.

"Oh, I—" His gaze flickered to the open blacktop and back to hers. He seemed to sink into her gaze, and Shannon's hand lifted and pressed against her heart like she was saying the Pledge of Allegiance.

"I've seen you around a few times," she said. "I'm going to have to ask you to leave." True regret lanced through her, because she'd very much like this man to stay, maybe come to her office where she'd close the door and learn more about him. She'd seen him at church with another cowboy from the horse ranch up the canyon and had learned everything she needed to know but his name. And Shannon didn't live in small-town Utah because she disliked cowboys.

Quite the opposite. Problem was, she'd dated every available man during the six years she'd been in Brush Creek, and she'd given up hope of finding someone here. Her disappointment that a transfer hadn't come through this year dried up. Very aware of how unreasonable she was being, she added, "And I think you should stay away. I don't want to have to call the police."

The man fell back a step, alarm entering his eyes. "No need for that. I'll go." He turned and walked away without looking back. A pang of renewed disappointment sang through Shannon, and she sighed as she turned back to the activity on the blacktop. Why did she run off every available man?

It didn't matter. She hadn't gotten a transfer this year, but she'd been at Brush Creek Elementary for six years. Next year would be number seven, and if she didn't get a transfer then, she'd know something was wrong with her performance.

But her parent and teacher surveys had been positive, and she'd never received a negative supervisor evaluation.

With her future almost certainly not in Brush Creek, she didn't need to worry so much about dating. But Shannon also knew she wasn't' getting any younger, and her biological clock seemed to be ticking in her ears louder and louder every day. She wanted a family and children—of her own. Her staff and students had always provided those things for her, and for a while there, Shannon thought that would be enough.

But she knew now that it wasn't. She wanted her own home, her own husband to come home to at night, her own children to cradle and cuddle and cater to.

She swallowed as a fourth grader ran toward her. "Miss Sharpe! Come see our hip hop dance." The excitement on the boy's face brought a smile to Shannon's face, and she moved as quickly as her heels would let her toward the fourth grade group, the pit in her stomach remaining no matter how much she enjoyed the children.

---

By the time Shannon finished work for the day, exhaustion consumed her. She unlocked her front door—she was possibly the only person in Brush Creek to lock their door—and exhaled as she entered.

At least she didn't have to come home to darkness and emptiness, as the early May evening still provided sunlight and her two dogs came trotting toward her, seemingly smiling and their tongues hanging out.

"Hey, guys." She put her keys and purse on the front table and bent down to rub her dogs. "Hey, Theo. Did you have a good day?" The curtain at the back of the house fluttered slightly in the wind, an indication that the short-haired Australian shepherd had opened the sliding glass door again.

Her goldendoodle nosed his way into the pat-down, and Shannon chuckled. "All right, Bear. I'll rub you too." The dog flopped on the ground and rolled onto his back, wanting his belly rubbed. "You big baby." She grinned at him, the reason why she locked the front door obvious. Neither of these dogs would bark or scare anyone who tried to break in. And Theo practically invited intruders in by opening the door so he could romp through the backyard.

Shannon straightened and started taking herself apart. First, the earrings came off. She massaged her sore lobes, vowing never to wear that particular pair again as they were too heavy. Then the multiple necklaces. The rings. The business jacket. The heels. Shannon took meticulous care putting every piece in place before she left the house, and it was a relief to just *be* in her own home.

She switched on the television in the living room and moved into the open kitchen to start dinner. She liked to cook just fine, but tonight, she went for easy. And easy meant a mango-peach protein shake on the back patio.

The neighbors were in their backyard and the shouts of children jumping on the trampoline met her ears, along with the scent of grilling hamburgers. Her stomach twisted and roared for meat instead of fruit. Theo and Bear went over to the fence and sat as if someone would accidentally drop a burger over it.

As if drawn by the panting dogs, Shannon's neighbor appeared over the top of the fence. She kept a utility chest there and stood on it when she wanted to talk to Shannon.

"Hey, you are home. Want to come over for dinner?" Ruth was the nicest person on the planet, and Shannon had developed a great friendship with her over the years.

"You don't even have to ask twice." Shannon stood with a grin and added, "Did you make potato salad?"

"Don't I always make potato salad when we have a cookout?"

Shannon grinned, stopped by the kitchen to dump out her uneaten shake, and slipped on some flip flops to go next door. She leashed the two dogs together and told them, "Don't pull. And no jumping," before walking around the fences and through the gate into Ruth's backyard. Her three kids bounced and called on the trampoline in the far corner, and her husband stood at the grill with an overly large spatula.

Ruth lounged in a chair at the patio table, and Shannon joined her, commanding the dogs to sit and wait.

"The dogs can go," she said, and Shannon unleashed them. Theo ran toward the trampoline, more enthralled with play, while Bear made a beeline for Clyde at the grill. The man laughed and rewarded Bear for his loyalty with a corner of bacon.

"Rough week?" Ruth asked, and Shannon opened her eyes. She hadn't even realized she'd closed them.

"May is a rough month," she said. "Everyone's done with school, the principal included." She flashed a weary smile at her friend. "How are things at the hospital?"

"Slow right now, surprisingly." Ruth wasn't wearing her scrubs today, which meant she hadn't worked. But she'd still know.

"That's good, I guess."

"Yeah." Ruth relaxed into her chair, and Shannon appreciated the silence between them on this Friday night.

"So, has Hannah come around?"

Shannon's muscles seized. "No." She didn't mean for

the word to come out like a gunshot, but it still did. "She's still mad at me."

Ruth shook her head and patted her hand. "I'm sorry."

Before last Labor Day, on a rough day like today, after a long week at school, Shannon wouldn't be sitting next door chatting with Ruth. She'd be on the phone with her sister, telling her all about the faculty meeting that had gone over by thirty minutes and the handsome man she'd run off this afternoon.

But Hannah hadn't answered any of Shannon's calls for months. "I honestly thought she'd be over it by now."

"Steve *was* her fiancée," Ruth said.

"Steve was a two-timing jerk who hit on me in my parents' backyard." Shannon set her arms across her chest, her internal organs dancing with apprehension, just like they had been every time she thought of the incident. Every time she relived telling Hannah. Every time she thought about calling her sister—which was everyday—to try to explain one more time.

Shannon had been hit on plenty of times, and she hadn't made a mistake with Steve, no matter what Hannah said. Steve's immediate absence after Shannon's accusations should've backed up her story, but Hannah only blamed her for Steve leaving as well.

Her heart squeezed too tight and she tried to make everything relax by exhaling. It sort of worked.

Ruth copied her and added, "So, no date tonight?"

Shannon groaned. "I'm sorta off men right now, after that last fiasco." She didn't mention the cowboy; hadn't dared to think too much about him at all. If she let herself, she'd find out his name and phone number and call him in for "extra questioning" herself.

"That wasn't a fiasco," Ruth said, having been privy to all the details.

"No? What would you call a man who dates a woman when he already has a girlfriend?"

"Unfortunate?"

Shannon scoffed. "Sure." She didn't want to dwell on the unpleasantness of her most recent attempt at dating. Just because the other woman lived two towns over didn't make her any less of his girlfriend, nor the very public confrontation at the diner any less humiliating. No one had asked Shannon out since, and it had been six months.

Not that Shannon usually let the men ask her out. She almost always made the first move, something she wasn't embarrassed about. She did wonder if sometimes she came off a little too powerful, too strong, too intimidating. She'd been told that in the past, but she wasn't quite sure how not to be like that.

"Heard you were askin' about Grant," Ruth said next, and Shannon sorely regretted this weekend barbeque.

"Who's Grant?" she asked.

"Cowboy up at Brush Creek. Only single one left."

"Black hair? Long sideburns?" Shannon's only hope was to play dumb, like she didn't know who Ruth was talking about.

"That's him."

"He's been hanging around my school," Shannon said. "That's the only reason I was trying to figure out who he was."

"Sure," Ruth said, in the most sarcastic tone possible.

"No really," Shannon insisted. "He was dating one of my teachers last year and clearly isn't over her. Poor guy."

Thankfully, Clyde saved her from having to explain further with an announcement of "Burgers are ready." He set a platter of cheese-topped burgers on the table, and Shannon had to restrain herself from lunging toward them.

At least she could soothe her weariness, her long week, and her loneliness with smoky beef, cheddar, and toasted bread.

---

Can he dig deep and rely on his faith and his Brush Creek cowboy friend to make a relationship with Shannon successful? Find out in **SCHOOLED BY THE COWBOY- now available in ebook, audiobook, and paperback!**

# Books in the Brush Creek Cowboy Romance Series:

**Brush Creek Cowboy (Book 1):** Former rodeo champion and cowboy Walker Thompson trains horses at Brush Creek Horse Ranch, where he lives a simple life in his cabin with his ten-year-old son. A widower of six years, he's worked with Tess Wagner, a widow who came to Brush Creek to escape the turmoil of her life to give her seven-year-old son a slower pace of life. But Tess's breast cancer is back...

Walker will have to decide if he'd rather spend even a short time with Tess than not have her in his life at all. Tess wants to feel God's love and power, but can she discover and accept God's will in order to find her happy ending?

**The Cowboy's Challenge (Book 2):** Cowboy and professional roper Justin Jackman has found solitude at Brush Creek Horse Ranch, preferring his time with the animals he trains over dating. With two failed engagements in his past, he's not really interested in getting his heart stomped on again. But when flirty and fun Renee Martin picks him up at a church ice cream bar--on a bet, no less--he finds himself more than just a little interested. His Gen-X attitudes are attractive to her; her Millennial behaviors drive him nuts. Can Justin look past their differences and take a chance on another engagement?

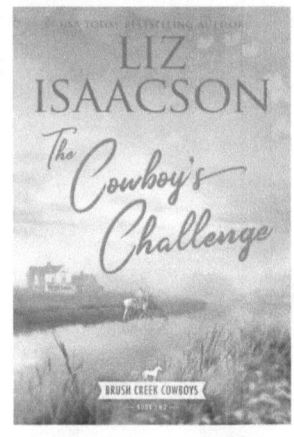

**A Cowboy Proposal (Book 3):** Ted Caldwell has been a retired bronc rider for years, and he thought he was perfectly happy training horses to buck at Brush Creek Ranch. He was wrong. When he meets April Nox, who comes to the ranch to hide her pregnancy from all her friends back in Jackson Hole, Ted realizes he has a huge family-shaped hole in his life. April is embarrassed, heartbroken, and trying to find her extinguished faith. She's never ridden a horse and wants nothing to do with a cowboy ever again. Can Ted and April create a family of happiness and love from a tragedy?

**A New Family for the Cowboy (Book 4):** Blake Gibbons oversees all the agriculture at Brush Creek Horse Ranch, sometimes moonlighting as a general contractor. When he meets Erin Shields, new in town, at her aunt's bakery, he's instantly smitten. Erin moved to Brush Creek after a divorce that left her  penniless, homeless, and a single mother of three children under age eight. She's nowhere near ready to start dating again, but the longer Blake hangs around the bakery, the more she starts to like him. Can Blake and Erin find a way to blend their lifestyles and become a family?

**The Cowboy and the Champion (Book 5):** Emmett Graves has always had a positive outlook on life. He adores training horses to become barrel racing champions during the day and cuddling with his cat at night. Fresh off her professional rodeo retirement, Molly Brady comes to Brush Creek Horse Ranch as Emmett's protege. He's not thrilled, and she's allergic to cats. Oh, and she'd like to stay cowboy-free, thank you very much. But Emmett's about as cowboy as they come.... Can Emmett and Molly work together without falling in love?

**Schooled by the Cowboy (Book 6):** Grant Ford spends his days training cattle—when he's not camped out at the elementary school hoping to catch a glimpse of his ex-girlfriend. When principal Shannon Sharpe confronts him and asks him to stay away from the school, the spark between them is instant and hot. Shannon's expecting a transfer very soon, but she also needs a summer outdoor coordinator—and Grant fits the bill. Just because he's handsome and everything Shannon's ever wanted in a cowboy husband means nothing. Will Grant and Shannon be able to survive the summer or will the Utah heat be too much for them to handle?

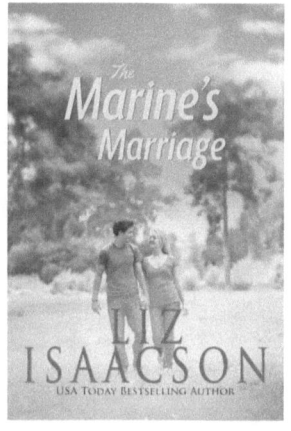

**The Marine's Marriage: A Fuller Family Novel - Brush Creek Cowboys Romance (Book 1):** Tate Benson can't believe he's come to Nowhere, Utah, to fix up a house that hasn't been inhabited in years. But he has. Because he's retired from the Marines and looking to start a life as a police officer in small-town Brush Creek. Wren Fuller has her hands full most days running her family's company. When Tate calls and demands a maid for that morning, she decides to have the calls forwarded to her cell and go help him out. She didn't know he was moving in next door, and she's completely unprepared for his handsomeness, his kind heart, and his wounded soul. **Can Tate and Wren weather a relationship when they're also next-door neighbors?**

**The Firefighter's Fiancé: A Fuller Family Novel - Brush Creek Cowboys Romance (Book 2):** Cora Wesley comes to Brush Creek, hoping to get some in-the-wild firefighting training as she prepares to put in her application to be a hotshot. When she meets Brennan Fuller, the spark between them is hot and  instant. As they get to know each other, her deadline is constantly looming over them, and Brennan starts to wonder if he can break ranks in the family business. He's okay mowing lawns and hanging out with his brothers, but he dreams of being able to go to college and become a landscape architect, but he's just not sure it can be done. **Will Cora and Brennan be able to endure their trials to find true love?**

**The Trooper's Treasure: A Fuller Family Novel - Brush Creek Cowboys Romance (Book 3):** Dawn Fuller has made some mistakes in her life, and she's not proud of the way McDermott Boyd found her off the road one day last year. She's spent a hard year wrestling with her choices and trying to fix them, glad for McDermott's acceptance and friendship. He lost his wife years ago, done his best with his daughter, and now he's ready to move on. **Can McDermott help Dawn find a way past her former mistakes and down a path that leads to love, family, and happiness?**

**The Detective's Date: A Fuller Family Novel - Brush Creek Cowboys Romance (Book 4):** Dahlia Reid is one of the best detectives Brush Creek and the surrounding towns has ever had. She's given up on the idea of marriage—and pleasing her mother—and has dedicated herself fully to her job. Which is great, since one of the most 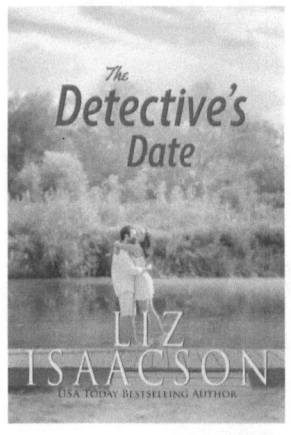 perplexing cases of her career has come to town. Kyler Fuller thinks he's finally ready to move past the woman who ghosted him years ago. He's cut his hair, and he's ready to start dating. Too bad every woman he's been out with is about as interesting as a lamppost—until Dahlia. He finds her beautiful, her quick wit a breath of fresh air, and her intelligence sexy. **Can Kyler and Dahlia use their faith to find a way through the obstacles threatening to keep them apart?**

**The Paramedic's Partner: A Fuller Family Novel - Brush Creek Cowboys Romance (Book 5):** Jazzy Fuller has always been overshadowed by her prettier, more popular twin, Fabiana. Fabi meets paramedic Max Robinson at the park and sets a date with him only to come down with the flu. So she convinces Jazzy to cut her hair and take her place on the date. And the spark between Jazzy and Max is hot and instant...if only he knew she wasn't her sister, Fabi.

Max drives the ambulance for the town of Brush Creek with is partner Ed Moon, and neither of them have been all that lucky in love. Until Max suggests to who he thinks is Fabi that they should double with Ed and Jazzy. They do, and Fabi is smitten with the steady, strong Ed Moon. **As each twin falls further and further in love with their respective paramedic, it becomes obvious they'll need to come clean about the switcheroo sooner rather than later...or risk losing their hearts.**

**The Chief's Catch: A Fuller Family Novel - Brush Creek Cowboys Romance (Book 6):** Berlin Fuller has struck out with the dating scene in Brush Creek more times than she cares to admit. When she makes a deal with her friends that they can choose the next man she goes out with, she didn't dream they'd pick surly Cole Fairbanks, the new Chief of Police.

His friends call him the Beast and challenge him to complete ten dates that summer or give up his bonus check. When Berlin approaches him, stuttering about the deal with her friends and claiming they don't actually have to go out, he's intrigued. As the summer passes, Cole finds himself burning both ends of the candle to keep up with his job and his new relationship. **When he unleashes the Beast one time too many, Berlin will have to decide if she can tame him or if she should walk away.**

# Books in the Horseshoe Home Ranch Romance Series:

**The Redesigned Ranch (Book 1):** Jace Lovell, still nursing a wounded heart after being jilted at the altar, has dedicated himself to becoming the best foreman at Horseshoe Home Ranch. When he decides to hire an interior designer to please the ranch owner's wife, he didn't expect to be faced with a familiar face from his past. **Can Belle's patience and faith help Jace find the path to forgiveness and lead them to discover their own slice of happily-ever-after?**

**Snowed in with the Cowboy (Book 2):** Sterling Maughan, once a renowned snowboarder, is in self-imposed exile at his family cabin after a tragic accident stole his career. Lost and without purpose, solitude is his only companion until an unexpected visitor disrupts his isolation. **Can Norah trust Sterling enough to let him into her life and give their unexpected and forbidden love a chance?**

**The Preacher's Daughter (Book 3):** Landon Edmunds, a cowboy born and bred, has had his rodeo dreams realized and then dashed by a career-ending injury. Back in his hometown working at Horseshoe Home Ranch, he yearns for a new beginning with a ranch of his own. His sights are set on buying a horse ranch to train rodeo horses, but his plans take a detour when his high school best friend, Megan Palmer, steps back into his life. **Will they choose to follow their hearts, or will they let true love slip through their fingers again?**

*Be sure to check out the spinoff series, the Brush Creek Cowboys romances after you read THE PREACHER'S DAUGHTER. Start with BRUSH CREEK COWBOY.*

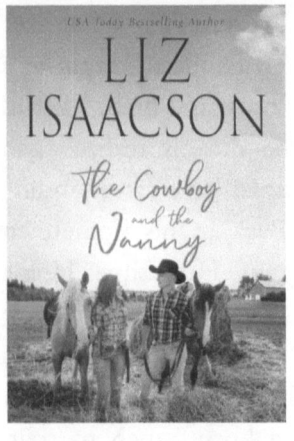

**The Cowboy and the Nanny(Book 4):** Twelve years ago, Owen Carr traded his roots and his sweetheart in Gold Valley for the bright lights of Nashville, where he found fame as a country music star. But when a tragic accident leaves him single-handedly raising his eight-year-old niece, Marie, he's forced to return home. Overwhelmed and out of his depth, Owen finds a lifeline in a most unexpected place. **As they mend bridges and explore the sparks that still sizzle between them, will they open their hearts to a second chance at love?**

**Right Cowboy, Right Time (Book 5):** Caleb Chamberlain, a fun-loving cowboy at Horseshoe Home Ranch, has spent the last five years wrestling with the ghosts of his past—a devastating breakup, alcoholism, and a near-fatal accident. Now, he's finally found solace in laughter and the rhythmic simplicity of ranch life. But a chance encounter with a familiar face threatens to upheave his newfound peace. **Can they navigate the shadows of the past to find their happily-ever-after?**

**Second Chance Family (Book 6):** Ty Barker has been living a carefree existence for the last thirty years. As friends around him found love and started families, Ty filled his time by giving horseback riding lessons and serving on a community service committee. But beneath the jovial surface, he's starting to feel the sting of loneliness. He knows he wants River Lee in his life—but the question is, can he navigate the delicate steps needed to make her stay with him?

**The Christmas Cowboy Competition (Book 7):** Archer Bailey has already had to yield one job to Emersyn "Emery" Enders. So when the opportunity of a cowhand job at Horseshoe Home Ranch presents itself, he keeps it to himself. Emery, whose temporary job is ending but whose responsibilities towards her physically disabled sister aren't, is left in the dark.

As the festive season unfolds, **will Emery and Archer navigate the complexities of the ranch, their close living arrangements, and their personal challenges to discover the love building between them? Or will their rivalry rob them of the greatest Christmas gift of all—true love?**

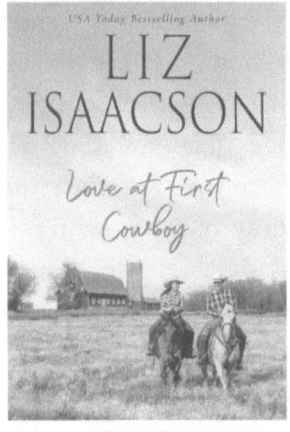

**Love at First Cowboy (Book 8):** Elliott Hawthorne, a career cowboy, has just witnessed his best friend and cabinmate forsake bachelorhood for matrimony. He'd be joyous if he weren't so green with envy. When a call about a family accident demands his presence, Elliott finds himself rushing from the ranch to his parents' house to see what's going on with his daddy, where he encounters the most stunning woman he's ever laid eyes on. **But as they encounter the complex dynamics of family responsibilities and personal desires, can their love-at-first-sight grow strong enough withstand the test of time?**

**Craving the Cowboy (Book 1):** Dwayne Carver is set to inherit his family's ranch in the heart of Texas Hill Country, and in order to keep up with his ranch duties and fulfill his dreams of owning a horse farm, he hires top trainer Felicity Lightburne. They get along great, and she can envision herself on this new farm—at least until her mother falls ill and she has to return to help her. Can Dwayne and Felicity work through their differences to find their happily-ever-after?

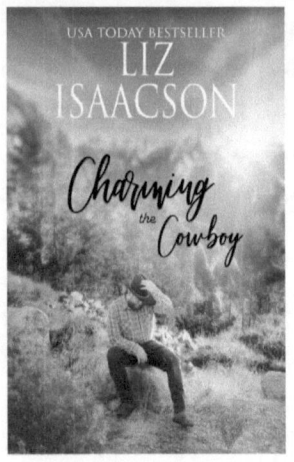

**Charming the Cowboy (Book 2):** Third grade teacher Heather Carver has had her eye on Levi Rhodes for a couple of years now, but he seems to be blind to her attempts to charm him. When she breaks her arm while on his horse ranch, Heather infiltrates Levi's life in ways he's never thought of, and his strict anti-female stance slips. Will Heather heal his emotional scars and he care for her physical ones so they can have a real relationship?

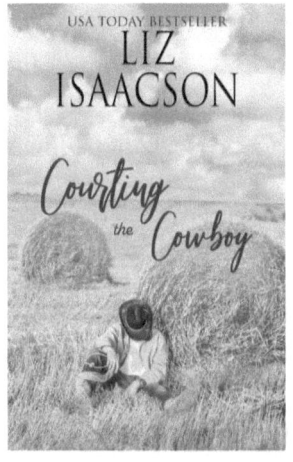

**Courting the Cowboy (Book 3):** Frustrated with the cowboy-only dating scene in Grape Seed Falls, May Sotheby joins Texas-Faithful.com, hoping to find her soul mate without having to relocate--or deal with cowboy hats and boots. She has no idea that Kurt Pemberton, foreman at Grape Seed Ranch, is the man she starts communicating with... Will May be able to follow her heart and get Kurt to forgive her so they can be together?

**Claiming the Cowboy, Royal Brothers Book 1 (Grape Seed Falls Romance Book 4):** Unwilling to be tied down, farrier Robin Cook has managed to pack her entire life into a two-hundred-and-eighty square-foot house, and that includes her Yorkie. Cowboy and co-foreman, Shane Royal has had his heart set on Robin for three years, even though she flat-out turned him down the last time he asked her to dinner. But she's back at Grape Seed Ranch for five weeks as she works her horseshoeing magic, and he's still interested, despite a bitter life lesson that left a bad taste for marriage in his mouth.

Robin's interested in him too. But can she find room for Shane in her tiny house--and can he take a chance on her with his tired heart?

**Catching the Cowboy, Royal Brothers Book 2 (Grape Seed Falls Romance Book 5):** Dylan Royal is good at two things: whistling and caring for cattle. When his cows are being attacked by an unknown wild animal, he calls Texas Parks & Wildlife for help. He wasn't expecting a beautiful mammologist to show up, all flirty and fun and everything Dylan didn't know he wanted in his life.

Hazel Brewster has gone on more first dates than anyone in Grape Seed Falls, and she thinks maybe Dylan deserves a second... Can they find their way through wild animals, huge life changes, and their emotional pasts to find their forever future?

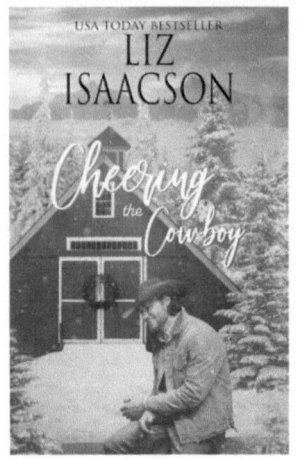

**Cheering the Cowboy, Royal Brothers Book 3 (Grape Seed Falls Romance Book 6):** Austin Royal loves his life on his new ranch with his brothers. But he doesn't love that Shayleigh Hatch came with the property, nor that he has to take the blame for the fact that he now owns her childhood ranch. They rarely have a conversation that doesn't leave him furious and frustrated--and yet he's still attracted to Shay in a strange, new way.

Shay inexplicably likes him too, which utterly confuses and angers her. As they work to make this Christmas the best the Triple Towers Ranch has ever seen, can they also navigate through their rocky relationship to smoother waters?

# Praise for Liz Isaacson

**Choosing the Cowboy (Book 7):** With financial trouble and personal issues around every corner, can Maggie Duffin and Chase Carver rely on their faith to find their happily-ever-after?

A spinoff from the #1 bestselling Three Rivers Ranch Romance novels, also by USA Today bestselling author Liz Isaacson.

# LAST CHANCE RANCH ROMANCE SERIES

**Last Chance Ranch (Book 1):** A cowgirl down on her luck hires a man who's good with horses and under the hood of a car. Can Hudson fine tune Scarlett's heart as they work together? Or will things backfire and make everything worse at Last Chance Ranch?

**Last Chance Cowboy (Book 2):** A billionaire cowboy without a home meets a woman who secretly makes food videos to pay her debts...Can Carson and Adele do more than fight in the kitchens at Last Chance Ranch?

**Last Chance Wedding (Book 3):** A female carpenter needs a husband just for a few days... Can Jeri and Sawyer navigate the minefield of a pretend marriage before their feelings become real?

**Last Chance Reunion (Book 4):** An Army cowboy, the woman he dated years ago, and their last chance at Last Chance Ranch... Can Dave and Sissy put aside hurt feelings and make their second chance romance work?

**Last Chance Lake (Book 5):** A former dairy farmer and the marketing director on the ranch have to work together to make the cow cuddling program a success. But can Karla let Cache into her life? Or will she keep all her secrets from him - and keep *him* a secret too?

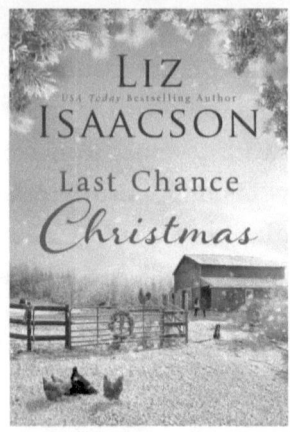

**Last Chance Christmas (Book 6):** She's tired of having her heart broken by cowboys. He waited too long to ask her out. Can Lance fix things quickly, or will Amber leave Last Chance Ranch before he can tell her how he feels?

# Books in the Christmas in Coral Canyon Romance series

**Graham (Book 1):** Graham Whittaker returns to Coral Canyon a few days after Christmas—after the death of his father. He takes over the energy company his dad built from the ground up and buys a high-end lodge to live in—only a mile from the home of his once-best friend, Laney McAllister. They were best friends once, but Laney's always entertained feelings for him, and spending so much time with him while they make Christmas memories puts her heart in danger of getting broken again...

**Eli (Book 2):** Since the death of his wife a few years ago, Eli Whittaker has been running from one job to another, unable to find somewhere for him and his son to settle. Meg Palmer is Stockton's nanny, and she comes with her boss, Eli, to the lodge, her long-time crush on the man no different in Wyoming than it was on the beach. When she confesses her feelings for him and gets nothing in return, she's crushed, embarrassed, and unsure if she can stay in Coral Canyon for Christmas. Then Eli starts to show some feelings for her too...

**Andrew (Book 3):** Andrew Whittaker is the public face for the Whittaker Brothers' family energy company, and with his older brother's robot about to be announced, he needs a press secretary to help him get everything ready and tour the state to make the announcements. When he's hit by a protest sign being carried by the company's biggest opponent, Rebecca Collings, he learns with a few clicks that she has the background they need. He offers her the job of press secretary when she thought she was going to be arrested, and not only because the spark between them in so hot Andrew can't see straight.

**Can Becca and Andrew work together and keep their relationship a secret? Or will hearts break in this classic romance retelling reminiscent of *Two Weeks Notice*?**

**Beau (Book 4):** Beau Whittaker has watched his brothers find love one by one, but every attempt he's made has ended in disaster. Lily Everett has been in the spotlight since childhood and has half a dozen platinum records with her two sisters. She's taking a break from the brutal music industry and hiding out in Wyoming while her ex-husband continues to cause trouble for her. When she hears of Beau Whittaker and what he offers his clients, she wants to meet him. Beau is instantly attracted to Lily, but he tried a relationship with his last client that left a scar that still hasn't healed...

**Can Lily use the spirit of Christmas to discover what matters most? Will Beau open his heart to the possibility of love with someone so different from him?**

**Todd (Book 5):** Todd Christopherson has just retired from the professional rodeo circuit and returned to his hometown of Coral Canyon. Problem is, he's got no family there anymore, no land, and no job. Not that he needs a job--he's got plenty of money from his illustrious career riding bulls.

Then Todd gets thrown during a routine horseback ride up the canyon, and his only support as he recovers physically is the beautiful Violet Everett. She's no nurse, but she does the best she can for the handsome cowboy. **Will she lose her heart to the billionaire bull rider? Can Todd trust that God led him to Coral Canyon...and Vi?**

**Liam (Book 6):** Rose Everett isn't sure what to do with her life now that her country music career is on hold. After all, with both of her sisters in Coral Canyon, and one about to have a baby, they're not making albums anymore.

Liam Murphy has been working for Doctors Without Borders, but he's back in the US now, and looking to start a new clinic in Coral Canyon, where he spent his summers.

When Rose wins a date with Liam in a bachelor auction, their relationship blooms and grows quickly. **Can Liam and Rose find a solution to their problems that doesn't involve one of them leaving Coral Canyon with a broken heart?**

**Finn (Book 7):** Her sons want her to be happy, but she's too old to be set up on a blind date...isn't she?

Amanda Whittaker has been looking for a second chance at love since the death of her husband several years ago. Finley Barber is a cowboy in every sense of the word. Born and raised on a racehorse farm in Kentucky, he's since moved to Dog Valley and started his own breeding stable for champion horses. He hasn't dated in years, and everything about Amanda makes him nervous.

**Will Amanda take the leap of faith required to be with Finn? Or will he become just another boyfriend who doesn't make the cut?**

**Zach (Book 8):** When Celia Abbott-Armstrong runs into a gorgeous cowboy at her best friend's wedding, she decides she's ready to start dating again.

But the cowboy is Zach Zuckerman, and the Zuckermans and Abbotts have been at war for generations.

Can Zach and Celia find a way to reconcile their family's differences so they can have a future together?

**Colton (Book 1):** All the maid at Whiskey Mountain Lodge wants for her birthday is a handsome cowboy billionaire. And Colton can make that wish come true—if only he hadn't escaped to Coral Canyon after being left at the altar...

**Wes (Book 2):** She broke up with him to date another man...who broke her heart. He's a former CEO with nothing to do who can't get her out of his head. Can Wes and Bree find a way toward happily-ever-after at Whiskey Mountain Lodge?

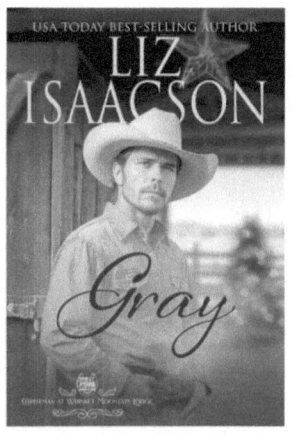

**Gray (Book 3):** She's best friends with the single dad cowboy's brother and has watched two friends find love with the sexy new cowboys in town. When Gray Hammond comes to Whiskey Mountain Lodge with his son, will Elise finally get her own happily-ever-after with one of the Hammond brothers?

**Cy (Book 4):** A cowboy billionaire beast, his new manager, and the Christmas traditions that soften his heart and bring them together.

**Ames (Book 5):** A cowboy billionaire cop who's a stickler for rules, the woman he pulls over when he's not even on duty, and the personal mandates he has to break to keep her in his life...

# SEVEN SONS RANCH IN THREE RIVERS ROMANCE™ SERIES

**Rhett (Book 1):** To save her business, she'll have to risk her heart. She needs a husband to be credible as a matchmaker. He wants to help a neighbor. **Will their fake marriage take them out of the friend zone?**

**Tripp (Book 2):** She needs a husband to keep her son. He's wanted to take their relationship to the next level, but she's always pushing him away. Will their trivial tie take them all the way to happily-ever-after?

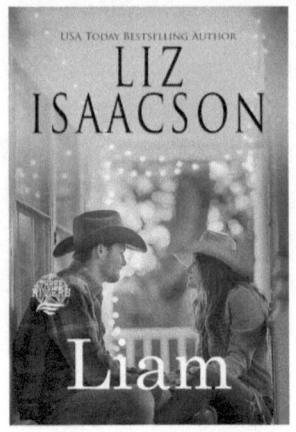

**Liam (Book 3):** She's desperate to save her ranch. He wants to help her any way he can. Will their invented I-Do open doors that have previously been closed and lead to a happily-ever-after for both of them?

**Jeremiah (Book 4):** He wants to prove to his brothers that he's not broken. She just wants him. Will a fake marriage heal him or push her further away?

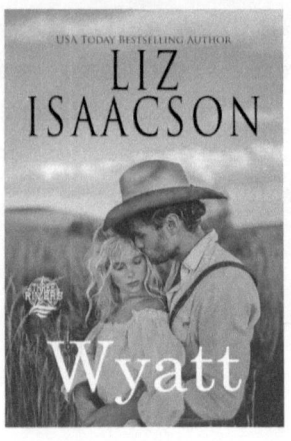

**Wyatt (Book 5):** To get her inheritance, she needs a husband. He's wanted to fly with her for ages. Can their pretend pledge turn into something real?

**Skyler (Book 6):** She needs a new last name to stay in school. He's willing to help a fellow student. Can this wanna-be wife show the playboy that some things should be taken seriously?

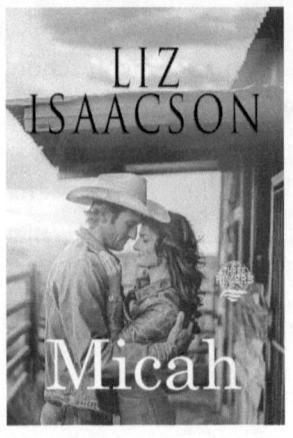

**Micah (Book 7):** They were just actors auditioning for a play. The marriage was just for the audition – until a clerical error results in a legal marriage. Can these two ex-lovers negotiate this new ground between them and achieve new roles in each other's lives?

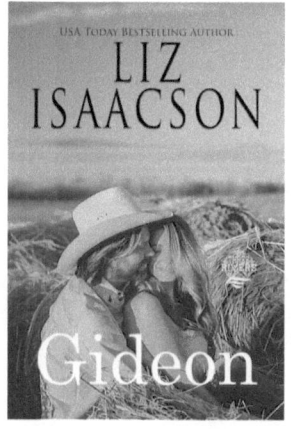

**Gideon (Book 8):** It's 1971, and Gideon Walker is on the cutting edge of all the technology coming out of Texas. He has big dreams and wants to make something of himself. Then he meets Penny Aarons, and everything changes. He only has eyes for her, but she's got plans and dreams of her own...

Read this origin romance for Momma and Daddy from the Seven Sons series today!

# About Liz

Liz Isaacson writes inspirational romance, usually set in Texas, or Wyoming, or anywhere else horses and cowboys exist. She lives in Utah, where she writes full-time, takes her two dogs to the park everyday, and eats a lot of veggies while writing. Find her on her website at feelgoodfiction-books.com

www.ingramcontent.com/pod-product-compliance
Lightning Source LLC
LaVergne TN
LVHW041634060526
838200LV00040B/1566